The
VALLEY
Is BRIGHT

THE VALLEY Is BRIGHT

The Nell Collins Story

NELL COLLINS
&
MARY BETH MOSTER

THOMAS NELSON PUBLISHERS
Nashville · Camden · New York

Second printing

Published in Nashville, Tennessee, by Thomas Nelson, Inc. and distributed in Canada by Lawson Falle, Ltd., Cambridge, Ontario.

Printed in the United States of America.

All Scripture quotations are from the King James Version of the Bible.

Illustrations in chapter IX are adapted from *The Search for Life* © 1978 by Nell Collins.

The quotation, "Pleasing God first, whether I feel like it or not" (p. 127), is from Jay Adams, *Ready to Restore*, (Philipsburg, N.J.: Presbyterian & Reformed, 1981), p. 30.

Library of Congress Cataloging in Publication Data

Collins, Nell.
  The valley is bright.

  1. Collins, Nell.   2. Christian biography—
United States.   3. Melanoma—Patients—United States—
Biography.   I. Moster, Mary Beth.   II. Title.
BR1725.M63A38   1983   209'.2'4 [B]   82-24562
ISBN 0-8407-5835-9

Acknowledgments

This story of my life is written with the single intention of exalting the person of Jesus Christ. He is the only Solution to the deepest heart needs of every human being. Life is full of problems, but God promises that we can have joy in the midst of them, based solely on what Christ has accomplished for us.

In this book it is my desire to minimize the human problems and maximize the divine solutions.

It would be impossible to personally thank all the people who have been important in my life. Naming everyone would be impractical, and it would be sad if anyone were excluded, so no real names will be used in this account except for the names of my parents, pastor, co-author, and myself. If any name used belongs to a real person, it is by coincidence.

Mary Beth would like to thank Norma Jean Coons, Jo Ann Hunt, and Kathy Schreiner for reading the manuscript and Shirley Hoke for typing it.

To all of those people who have loved me, encouraged me, and taught me the things of the Lord and His faithfulness, I thank you so very much. You are part of my life and this story.

Nell Collins

The
VALLEY
Is BRIGHT

I

The paper robe crinkled under me as I lay on the black examination table with my backside up and my face to the wall.

I could see the small table with the doctor's supplies on it, and as a nurse, I mentally checked off the equipment: syringe, hypodermic needles, antiseptic lotion, alcohol, biopsy jars . . . biopsy jars!

Those jars reminded me why I was there.

Only a week before I had been making a notation in a patient's chart at my post at the nurse's station in the hospital, when one of the doctors came to my floor on his rounds.

"Oh, Dr. Greene," I called, "I don't want to bother you, but there's something I'd like to ask you." As head nurse of the Constant Care Unit, I knew Dr. Greene well. Because he was a good friend, I felt that he would not mind a "hallway consultation."

"You may think I'm silly to even mention this," I said, "but, you see, I've got a couple of moles on my back that seem to be kinda itching." Dr. Greene gave me one of his Marcus Welby glances. "I checked them out in the mirror last night," I continued, "but I can't tell if they're weird or not."

"Well, let's take a look," he said.

He spoke casually as he inspected the moles, but furrows of concern grooved his forehead.

"It's probably nothing," he said, "but just the same I want you to see Dr. Fitzpatrick, the dermatologist, and have him examine them. Remember the old cliche: Better safe than sorry."

Dr. Fitzpatrick scrutinized the moles the next day, and removed them immediately. I carried them in biopsy jars to the hospital lab to be examined chemically and microscopically. Knowing from my experience as a nurse that most moles are ordinary and harmless, I thought, *Surely they are okay.*

As I lay on the examination table seven days later, waiting for Dr. Fitzpatrick to remove the stitches, I smiled, recalling our first encounter the previous week. He had bounced into the room with cheerful conversation, and we bantered in the friendly way of two medical people in a routine situation. This time he came into the room quietly, too quietly. He did not utter a sound, and neither did I. Silently he snipped at the black sutures on my back. Then he said it:

"I'm sorry, Nell." He seemed to search for the words. "I'm afraid one of those moles was a malignant melanoma."

Malignant? Melanoma? My head reeled. *CANCER! It can't be!* My heart pounded fiercely. I could feel each beat pulsate against the table. The doctor continued snipping and talking. I tried to concentrate on what he was saying, but that word kept spinning in my head. *Cancer! CANCER! No, No! It can't be.*

"You'll have to make arrangements for surgery right away, Nell," he said gently. "Your surgery will be extensive, and you'll need a skin graft. We'll have to act quickly."

The room started whirling.

This can't be happening! I'm the nurse; I take care of sick people. I don't get sick! I can't have cancer!

Finally, groping my way to my car, I felt hot tears streaming down my face. As I drove around the interstate to my apartment, the highway blurred before me. I felt as if a madman were holding a gun to my head. I began sobbing uncontrollably.

Cancer, cancer! Me, with CANCER! I pulled over to the side of the road and wept bitterly. I can't even remember driving the rest of the way home.

Somehow I found myself at the parking space in front of my apartment. The brick colonial townhouse looked empty and forlorn. The morning sunshine was gone, and grey clouds shrouded the sky. *The inside of my body,* I thought, *is crawling with melanoma cells. I'm unclean! Unclean with malignancy!* The thought revolted me. I felt as though a time bomb were ticking inside my body, ready to explode and blow my life away.

Malignant melanoma. Even the words sounded ominous. I stumbled into my apartment and looked up the disease in my nursing textbooks. "Malignant," of course, was another word for cancer. "Melanoma" described the type of cancer which usually begins in the pigmented skin cells called *melanocytes.* The text told me what I dreaded: *potential for invasion and metastasis!* This was not a simple skin cancer; it could deeply penetrate the body and travel quickly. I could almost feel the malignant cells pulsing through my bloodstream, taking control, establishing new tumors. If that were true, I could die within a few weeks or months.

The telephone seemed my lifeline. *If I could just talk to somebody who would tell me it's not true!*

"Mom?" I cried into the telephone. "Oh, Mom!" I sobbed and couldn't speak for a few minutes. "Mom, I've got malignant melanoma, and people die with that. Mom, I'm going to die!"

"Wait, Nelia Anne," she said in a frightened voice. "Wait just a minute. Calm down. Now start all over. What do you have?"

I tried to explain but couldn't find the words. "I'll talk to you later, Mom."

Then I called my friend Peggy. She came over and tried to pray for me, but I couldn't concentrate. "We just have to trust the Lord," she said.

"Trust the Lord?" I screamed. "Don't you realize I have malignant melanoma? How can you trust the Lord when you're *dying*?"

I wanted to pray, but I just couldn't get control of myself. *God, oh God! It can't be true. I'm too young to die.*

I was 29 years old.

Amazingly, that day, etched so clearly in my mind, happened more than ten years ago. I had no way of knowing in that time of panic, that the next decade would turn out to be the most exciting, fulfilling, and joyous of my life. The Lord has worked faithfully in my own life to show me that through Him, and only through Him, no matter what the circumstances of life, it is *possible* to have *peace* in the depths of the soul.

That day, as I was walking "through the valley of the shadow of death," I did not know that the valley can be *bright*, when experiencing God's love, peace, and presence in the midst of tragedy and crisis.

I could not have guessed, when the doctor told me I had cancer in my body, that God had a plan to use my cancer to help hundreds, then thousands, of other cancer patients.

If someone had suggested that I would eventually devote my remaining earthly life to ministering to the needs of cancer patients, I would have said, "No way. I can't handle my own cancer, let alone anybody else's."

If someone had told me that I would someday teach teams of lay people in local churches all over the country the principles of dealing with people in crisis, I would have thought they were crazy.

Back at my apartment, I had to wait three endless days before going to the hospital for surgery. After Peggy left I locked myself in my apartment and tried to pull myself together.

The fears were so overwhelming I could not even identify them. The fear of death overshadowed the others, but
my thoughts ran wild: *Will I have enough insurance to take
care of me through the end? What if I run out of money? How
will Mom be able to handle my suffering and death?*

Then an even more horrible thought occurred to me.
*What if I don't die right away? What if I become an invalid and
have to go to a nursing home or something?* The thought was
too awful.

As I lay in bed unable to cry any more and equally
unable to sleep, I began to think about my life. Events of
my childhood whirled through my memory, and I
thought about my teenage years, my life as a nurse, and
especially my relationship with God. Somehow I wanted
to make sense of the crazy quilt of my life before it ended.

■ ■

As my thoughts convulsed through my mind, I remembered the day Daddy pulled the old blue Plymouth close to the curb in front of our "new house." I peeked out the back window analyzing the white frame building critically, unemotionally. Eleven years old, I was experienced in moving.

The house had a plainness about it that seemed to be reserved for those in the Lord's work—adequate, but ordinary.

Why does it have to be so blah? I thought resentfully. *Christians can't ever have anything really sharp.*

Even my name was boring. My mother had named me Nelia Anne after her favorite author, Nelia Gardner White, and also after my father, Neil. *Nelia Anne. What an out-of-date, frumpy old name. Sounds like doilies and tatting,* I thought. How wonderful it would be to have an "in" name—something like *Jennifer* or *Judy*—and live in a fancy house and dress like the little girls in the Montgomery Ward catalogue. We never had money for anything, let alone clothes. *Oh, well,* I thought. *I'm too fat to look good in pretty clothes, anyway.*

Money was not available to go out for dinner or even for an ice cream cone, and I hated not having anything and not being able to do anything. Then I felt guilty for being so selfish. Now we were moving into another unremarkable house in a town that looked like all the others.

"Not even one person here to greet you," Daddy commented bitterly.

"We shall manage," Mom replied.

"As you say, 'the Lord provides,'" Daddy muttered, his voice laced with sarcasm.

"Quiet, Neil!" Mom said harshly. "The children . . ."

"The children! Always the children." He paused uncomfortably. "I don't know why we had to move again. Every time we just get settled in one place, you have to get transferred."

Mom tightened her mouth in the determined set we knew so well.

"If God tells you to do something," she said dramatically, "then you *do* it. You don't ask why."

Daddy turned his head. He knew he could not compete in an argument against both Mom and God.

Those kinds of conversations puzzled me. I'd never heard God tell us to move. He'd never said the first word to me.

By this time Daddy was standing beside the car, scratching his head and looking bewildered. Mom opened her car door, looked back at me, and said, "Nelia Anne, watch your baby brother. I'm going to find out how we can get a key." She marched with determination to the parsonage, and when she found the door locked she looked under the mat and in the mailbox. Undaunted, she briskly made her way to the house next door. She looked every bit in charge. Her close-cropped dark hair and plain black dress gave her the look of one in authority.

I had no doubt about her being "in charge." As she was a "lady preacher," everyone looked up to her and sought her advice. None of the church members seemed to think it was unusual that Mom was the preacher, and I just accepted it as a natural part of my childhood.

Daddy leaned against the dusty car, eyes downcast, with his hands shoved deep into his pockets. "You'd think they'd have somebody here to unlock the door," he grumbled.

My little brother slept soundly and I wriggled restlessly, eager to explore my new surroundings. My brother looked okay to me, so I slipped quietly out the back door of the car.

The church was on the other side of the parsonage, and like the house, it was a simple, white frame structure. I bounded up the front steps and, surprisingly, found the door unlocked. The brass handle felt cool as I pulled open the door, and I tiptoed into the sanctuary. The sun filtered in through a single stained glass window, and I looked around our new church, trying to imagine if this town would be any different from the other places we had lived. I thought about how lonely I was and how far I felt from the God my mother talked about so constantly.

"Nelia! Nelia Anne, where are you?"

Oh, no! I thought. *I'm supposed to be watching my brother!*

I scrambled out of the church and down the steps and almost ran the other way when I saw Mother standing there, switch in hand. Daddy, typically, was nowhere in sight.

By this time the whole neighborhood was watching. The preacher's kid was going to get it, right in front of everyone. My face flamed with fury as the switch snapped against my legs. I was too humiliated to look at the children. They would never want to be my friends now.

I found it would be one more lonely, lonely house.

A few days later I went to the street corner and sat on the curb, hoping to find someone, anyone, to take away the loneliness. A group of children breezed down the sidewalk on roller skates, laughing easily with one another. They stopped and stared at me.

A bigger kid said, "You new?"

"Uh-huh." I looked down at the curb, hoping they would include me but sure they wouldn't.

"Where do ya live?" he asked.

I pointed to the parsonage, and they all looked at each other knowingly.

"Ya got skates?"

I nodded my head, but they shrugged; then they wheeled on down the sidewalk. *Why don't they want me to skate with them?* I wondered. *Is it because I'm a preacher's kid? Or is it because I'm fat?*

I went home and searched for something to eat. Whenever I felt lonely and blue, all I wanted was food. It didn't take long to find a plate of brownies and polish them off. *These brownies will make me even fatter,* I thought miserably, *but I don't care!*

I hated myself for being fat, but it seemed that the more disgusted I was with my weight, the more I ate.

One time we had a candy sale at school. I bought a two-pound box of chocolates and ate all of them during lunch hour. Another time I sneaked into my room with a whole pound of bologna, a carton of Coke, and a loaf of bread. I gulped it all down and hid the "evidence" under the bed.

I'd always been fat. My brother, infuriatingly skinny, could eat whatever he wanted. At dinnertime Mom constantly encouraged him to eat more, but would say to me, "That's enough, Nelia. You've eaten too much the way it is."

Mom seemed always to be preaching at me about something, and as I grew older I wondered how she happened to become a preacher in the first place. Her answer, typically, was brief and to the point.

"I was *called*. God called me."

"From Heaven?"

"Well," she gave me one of her wry smiles, "it was something like that. When I was eighteen years old, back in 1925, I worked in an office as a typist. At the end of the day, I was walking home when I saw a billboard. All of a sudden, I looked up at the sign, and it said 'GO PREACH.' It scared me half to death."

"What did you do?"

"Well, being so young, I didn't know what to do, so I went to the minister of our little church. He thought I was coming to tell him I wanted to get married or something. When he heard of my experience, he looked as dumb-founded as I was, handed me a book on church doctrine, and wished me luck. I had thirty-five cents in my pocket, so I just started preaching in little country churches for whatever I could get and went to school as much as I could during the week."

She had been preaching for nine years when she met my father.

"I met him at a revival," she once said. "He could sing like the very angels of heaven. When he was on stage, all attention was riveted on him, and his singing could melt the hardest of hearts. I thought he would be the perfect husband because he was in the Lord's work."

I noticed the lines etched on her brow and saw the deep disappointment in her eyes.

Mom was right. When he was singing, he was beauti-ful. The sweetness of his songs brought tears to my eyes. In the spotlight he glowed as though someone had turned on a switch inside him and, suddenly, he was endearing the audience with his gracious and godly manner.

But offstage he was different; he reserved his charm for the crowds. At home he rarely talked. His darkly quiet and sullen moods kept him emotionally removed from the rest of us. He would sit in his chair in the corner, reading or writing in his voluminous diary. At the first sign of disruption in the household, he would go for a long walk to escape it. Consequently, Mom was left "in charge" of us children.

Sometimes I found Mom washing dishes and weeping, tears streaming down her cheeks, unable to express her sorrow. I did not realize until much later that she had wanted the "ideal Christian home," and reality was far from her expectations. Many years later I realized that all she had wanted was a little of the "charming" Daddy; instead, she was left alone, wishing he would pay some attention to her, wishing he would love her. Of course, no one knew about the undercurrent of unrest in our home.

The Bible passages referring to God as Father confused me. To me, a father went "on the road" during the revival season, and, generally speaking, we were glad to see him go. The house had less tension when he was gone. In my experience, a father would withdraw if pestered by a childish request or broken toy. "Don't bother me. Go ask your mother," was the standard reply.

Mom not only made the decisions, she administered all discipline. One Sunday when I was just a toddler, I had squirmed in the church pew and talked out loud during one of Mom's services. She stopped in the middle of the sermon, grabbed me, and took me up to the front of the church. She pulled out the pulpit chair and turned it so it would face the wall. Without a word, she sat me soundly in the chair, then went right on preaching. I poked an index finger into each ear and perched there, elbows sticking out, throughout the remainder of the service. *If I can't talk*, I thought, *I'm not gonna listen either!*

On another summer day my mother entertained the Missionary Circle meeting at the parsonage. She dressed me in a clean white pinafore, and all the ladies oohed and ahhed about what a cute little girl I was. Before long, however, the ladies started chattering about other things which I found quite dull, so I slipped outside and found a little tan kitten and a can of red paint in the garage. I came back into the house with a red cat and a red pinafore. The ladies didn't consider *that* cute at all.

Failure followed me like a shadow. I wanted to "do right," and I tried to please my mom. But no matter how hard I tried, I always seemed to botch it. I disappointed myself, and I was sure that I disappointed God, too.

Sometimes, in the quiet darkness of the night, my thoughts would turn to meeting God someday. "SORRY, NELIA," God boomed in my dreams, "YOU WERE AL-MOST GOOD ENOUGH, BUT NOT QUITE." Then He would slam the door to Heaven in my face. Eternity frightened me.

It seemed that my problems could be solved by making a "commitment" to God. My mother extended an invitation to "go to the altar" at the conclusion of the services. I figured that God must be at the altar. And anyway, I didn't want to let my parents down in front of all the church people.

After all, I thought to myself, *what will people think if the preacher's daughter doesn't go to the altar?*

Again and again I went down the aisle. I said all the words that I had learned I should say. I was baptized. I acted like a Christian, talked like a Christian, and looked like a Christian. If anyone had asked me if I were a Christian, I would have said, "Of course I am! My mother's the preacher, for goodness sake!"

But inside, all I knew was emptiness.

We moved three more times before we settled into the town where I would finish high school.

School had been in session several weeks at the time of our move, and, once again, I felt conspicuous as the "new kid in town."

The rural community reminded me of other places we had lived, but the high school building looked big and overwhelming. I approached the massive doors with excitement, but when I looked down I saw my petticoat hanging out from my gathered cotton skirt. *Why didn't I take the time to iron this wrinkled skirt?* I thought. I never thought about things like that until it was too late.

My sensible brown shoes looked matronly, my socks were stretched and baggy, and my hair! Mom always cut it short and simple. The object was not to be attractive, just neat. Pretty was "worldly," the way I understood it. God probably liked dowdiness, but I hated it, especially on me.

A pretty girl, with smooth blonde hair curled in a flawless page boy, came up behind me. She wore hose and loafers, a madras plaid shirt, and had a navy blue cardigan sweater tied casually around her shoulders.

Even her fingernails were neatly trimmed and manicured. I knew without looking that mine were jagged and torn from my biting them off.

She probably weighed about eighty pounds, and she came up to my shoulders. I felt like a buffalo.

She looked at my metal lunch box, and I noticed she didn't have one.

"Oh," she laughed, "*nobody* brings lunch to school. We all quit that in junior high. We all walk downtown to the corner drugstore for lunch."

She joined a group of laughing girls, and I sneaked in the door, trying to hide my stupid lunch box. Every day for two weeks I refused to buy milk at school so I would have enough money to eat downtown.

The kids walked together in groups of three or four, and I felt conspicuous walking alone. The drugstore was six or seven blocks away, and we had to walk past several stores with big glass windows. In the reflection, I looked like a fat slob. *No wonder nobody likes me,* I thought.

At the drugstore, the kids were standing three and four deep at the soda fountain, and some were smoking cigarettes, trying to look "real cool." Another group huddled around the paperback book rack. I heard one girl say, "Check out page 147 in this one," then they all giggled. I felt a little wild just being there.

I coated my breaded tenderloin with mayonnaise, and squiggled catsup all over my french fries. The malt was so thick I had to eat it with a spoon. I loved it.

On the way back to school the giggling girls let me join them. I refused to stare at my image in the store windows. *I'll never look at my reflection again,* I determined, *I'll not let what I look like spoil my fun.* I wanted these girls to like me. I laughed shrilly and chattered gaily to cover my lack of confidence. They thought I was "tons" of fun.

My euphoria lasted only until gym class; then I was abruptly reminded that I was three times bigger than anyone else.

As soon as the bell rang, I dashed into the locker room, hoping to be able to change into my uniform before the other girls got there. The smell of sour sweat in the locker room always slightly nauseated me, but I hurried in there, fearful that someone would see me half dressed with my rolls of fat in plain sight. I always tried to be first or last so no one could see me. I lied to the teacher about showering, too. She must have known that I never took one, but she let me get by with it. I guess she felt sorry for me.

We wore cute one-piece maroon jump suits for gym. The other girls, with their slim little bodies, looked just darling. Mine was way too tight, and I looked like a Mack truck.

My fat kept me from being good at anything athletic. That day we were playing half-court basketball, and within minutes I was gasping for breath. Running was hard for me, shooting the ball impossible. My lack of coordination was more than embarrassing.

I tried to make up for my general failure in life by doing reasonably well in school.

One day the Latin teacher stopped me after class. She was the serious, intellectual type, but had a certain kindness about her. I liked her because she encouraged me.

"Nelia Anne," she said, "I've noticed you have an ability in Latin. You grasp the vocabulary quickly. Do you know what you want to do when you get out of high school?"

I felt my face redden, and my heart pounded. "Yes, ma'am," I said, "I want to be a nurse. I've always wanted to be a nurse."

"Well, you'll make a good one," she said with a smile.

I'd wanted to be a nurse since I was a little girl. Missionaries who had been in faraway and glamorous places visited us frequently. They impressed me with their exciting stories of heathen savages. When I was younger, I had thought maybe I, too, could impress people if I became a missionary-nurse. But now I was growing disillusioned with religion. It seemed like such a fakery. It would be enough to be a nurse; I would drop the missionary part. Going to nurse's training also meant I could leave home. *I can't wait!* I thought.

I felt like a miserable failure as a Christian. It seemed impossible to be the 100 percent perfect Christian everyone thought I should be, so why try? Who wanted to go through life pretending? I wanted to get away from my old-fashioned religious background. I wanted to be a nurse, but even more, I wanted to get out on my own and not have to conform to the Christian "mold" everyone expected me to fit.

Most of the time I did enjoy our church youth group which provided nearly all of my "social" outings. I looked forward to meeting with the other ten or twelve teenagers in the group.

One night, however, the youth group planned a wiener roast and hayride. I dreaded some of our activities because the other kids would pair off, and I was too fat, I thought, to have a boyfriend.

We all met at the church and then went in cars to a nearby farm. We climbed in the hay wagons and the farmer pulled us with a tractor out to a campsite along a river bank.

The night was cool, the autumn air crisp. The couples, by now, were holding hands and whispering to each other. I felt very alone.

"Here, let me help," I said to Mr. Moore, our youth leader. I brought him wood from the wagon. He piled the pieces of wood in a circle and surrounded the pile with rocks. I brought him matches and watched as the blaze took hold.

Mrs. Moore spread a piece of oilcloth on the picnic table, and I helped her arrange the hot dogs, baked beans, potato salad, and marshmallows. I drank several soft drinks and ate a bag of potato chips while helping her. The youth leaders seemed to enjoy me; adults usually did. I'd always felt more comfortable around grownups than with kids my own age.

Mrs. Moore talked with me about Mike's new girlfriend. Mike was the sharpest guy in the youth group, and I was happy if he even said "hello" to me.

"Don't you think they look cute together?" Mrs. Moore was saying. They did. They really did. I went over to the fire and speared a couple more hotdogs, held them over the fire until they were black, then covered them with mustard and relish before wolfing them down. I hated myself for feeling resentment toward Mike and his cute little girlfriend, but maybe some roasted marshmallows would make me feel better. I sat all alone by the fire and ate until it was time to go.

Later, when I was a senior in high school, I had my very first date. Allen, a boy in our youth group, asked me to go with him to one of our parties. I discovered that even a fat girl could have a boyfriend! We began to go out regularly. Both of us were somewhat lonely, and neither had very much self-confidence, but we laughed and clowned around together. He was the first person my own age who really seemed to like me. Everyone understood we were "going steady."

Before graduation night, a girlfriend and I talked about the class party. We were going to a dinner and reception at the nicest restaurant in town and we planned what we would wear. "Nelia Anne," she said, "I think Allen wants to get married. He keeps talking about getting a job and finding an apartment."

"Married! You're kidding!" I gasped. "I'm only seventeen years old. I'm too young to get married. And, anyway, I'm going to be a nurse. I've always wanted to be a nurse. I can't be a nurse if I get married."

"Allen doesn't want you to be a nurse. He just wants to get married."

I said it slowly, emphatically, *"I am going to be a nurse."*

At the senior class party, Allen said, "I guess you're serious about going off to become a nurse. That's okay if it's what you want."

I didn't see much of him that summer.

IV

"Your name, please?"

The girl at the registration desk for nursing school chomped on her chewing gum and looked very bored. She didn't know the importance of her quesion, for I had decided to eliminate from my life *Nelia* and all the fossilized ideas that name represented to me.

"I'm Nell," I said, feeling a little strange. It was the first time I didn't call myself *Nelia*. "I'm Nell Collins," I said with an air of sophistication, I hoped. "I'm an incoming freshman."

She yawned. Her look told me she had seen lots of girls like me that day. Although trying to be "cool," I was still a scared little girl who had never been away from home.

Looking at the huge hospital and all of the buildings associated with it, I was thrilled to be part of such a big, metropolitan operation. The doctors and nurses looked so self-confident and superior. Maybe changing my name would make me more like them.

It was August 31, 1959, my eighteenth birthday, and *Nelia* no longer existed. My name was *Nell* to everyone I met that day.

Nursing school, I silently vowed, *will be a whole new beginning for me. People will never know what kind of person I really am.*

The freshman girls lived in a building near the hospital

used at that time for a dormitory. My room looked like all the others: a single twin bed, a desk, a chair, and a couple of shelves.

The glossy green walls gave no hint of homeyness. We walked for miles through the various wings of the hospital on the same drab but servicable tile that covered the floors of our rooms. *But at least,* I thought, *I'm out on my own, getting a brand new start.*

It didn't take long for the bubble to burst. Sadly, *Nelia* came right along to school with me. My new name did not change *me.* Some of the girls started calling me "Nellie." That was almost as bad as "Nelia." On that first Monday of school I agonized through a grim reminder that I could not get away from myself.

I had applied for a scholarship a few months earlier and on the application blank was a section for personal information. I cringed when I had to write, "Height: 5'7", Weight: 200 lbs." They denied me the scholarship, telling me, tactfully of course, that I was too fat to be a nurse. Fat girls, in those days, couldn't even *go* to nursing school, let alone get scholarships. In order to be admitted to school, I'd have to lose 50 pounds by the time school started.

On Monday, I trudged to the health office for the official "weigh in." Starving myself all summer, I had lost about 30 pounds. Not nearly enough. *Maybe they won't even let me stay in school,* I worried.

Several other fat girls were jammed in the health office that morning, looking as miserable and dejected as I felt.

A skinny nurse came into the room. Obviously she was going to weigh us. *I'll bet they picked her just to be mean,* I thought glumly. We stood in a big (I mean *big*) line, and one by one she weighed us and announced our fate. When my turn came, she studied my chart, then looked up and down my frame.

"I see you were to have lost 50 pounds."

"Yes, ma'am."

"Well, step up on the scales here and we'll see how you did . . . hmmm . . . looks like 170."

She was not impressed with my weight loss.

Heavy silence. Some calculating. Tsk. Tsk.

"Since you have lost some of the weight, you will be enrolled in school on probation until you get down to 150 pounds. You will come here every Monday morning to be weighed."

So I had the dubious distinction of being on the "fat list" with the other girls on probation. It reinforced my opinion of myself. *I am a slob. I'll never be anything but a slob, so why try?*

Every week we fatties went through the same routine. We refused to eat a bite on Saturday or Sunday, then after being weighed on Monday, some of us went to the Dairy Queen for a banana split. Or two.

My status of "on probation" lasted the entire three years of school. The trick was to lose enough weight to stay in school. Then it would be time to celebrate by "pigging out." Who cared if the pounds went back on again?

They issued student uniforms to us. Most of the girls looked so crisp in them, so neat and clean and *slender*. The first time I tried mine on, my heart sank. Somehow I thought it would do more for me.

The blue and white striped cotton dress buttoned up the front. Even a size eighteen was too tight for me and I had to pull hard to get the middle button fastened. *Hope it doesn't pop,* I thought. The dress had a stiffly starched collar and cuffs that were detachable and a white bibbed pinafore with a wide waistband that buttoned in back.

By the time I got the whole contraption on, the perspiration dripped down my face and the under-dress hung limply. The pinafore wilted and when I bent over to tie my shoes (an effort in itself, believe me), the waistband rolled and looked as though I had taken a nap in it. My greatest disappointment was that the uniform did not transform me into the professional-looking nurse I had hoped to be.

Before even the first semester was completed, I got a letter from Mom. *Funny how little I even think about home*, I mused as I tore open the envelope. She chattered on and on about various people in town. She was no longer preaching; she took early retirement on disability for her heart problems. My brother had started high school, and she said he was fine. Daddy had also dropped out of the ministry; he now worked in a warehouse for a local publishing firm. He still took long walks and seemed to stay away from home as much as possible. Mom sounded lonely.

Then, near the end, she added, almost as an afterthought, "By the way, dear, Allen's engaged to Lillian Thompson. She was in your class, wasn't she? Well, they are going to live right here in town. I saw him a day or two ago, and he seems very happy."

My self-esteem plummeted. My first and only boyfriend almost couldn't wait until I got out of town before marrying someone else.

In tears I called Mom collect, something I had not done before.

As usual, she assessed the situation succinctly: "What did you expect him to do? Join the foreign legion?"

I realized I needed to concentrate on my studies. After all, I gave up getting married to become a nurse, but I would never be a nurse unless I could get through school.

The academic requirements of school confounded me. Being undisciplined and unorganized, I usually felt "covered up" with homework and had to cram for tests.

One night I lugged a huge pile of books out to the lounge. Someone had put on coffee and ordered donuts. We were having a mid-term examination in pharmacology and I agonized over how far behind I was in reading for chemistry class.

Shoveling in another donut and reaching for my sixth

cup of coffee, I chastised myself for procrastinating. *Why had I wasted all that time with coke-and-pizza parties this week? Why did I have to goof off again?*

At two o'clock in the morning I could no longer concentrate, but all that coffee made it impossible to sleep. I lay in bed, hating myself for getting so far behind, paralyzed with fear that I would not make it. *What if I can't hack it? What if I flunk out?*

I joined a fellowship for Christian nurses, because I liked the girls in the group. They were the sharpest and smartest girls, and I wanted to be associated with them. I even sang with two other girls in a trio of Christian nurses. The piano player, Sally Williams, became my best friend.

The girls at school seemed to be divided into two main groups: the "Christian" girls and the "wild" girls. I wanted to belong to both groups. I wanted to be wild, but I wanted the Christian girls to like me. I wanted to be good, but I also wanted to be bad.

Most of my "badness" in school was a result of my horrible feelings of inferiority. I felt that everybody was sharper than I, and I tried to hide those feelings by becoming "notorious" for testing all the rules and fighting the system.

Notices from the Board of Infractions frequently were stuffed in my mail box. "Infractions notices" were sent for things like making noise in the hall, getting in late (those were the days when girls in school had hours), screeching during study hours, and staying up after the set time for bed. Sometimes I was ordered to make a personal appearance before the dean.

My antics didn't seem too bad to me until I got caught. Then feelings of failure crushed me. I felt no good, unable to do anything positive with my life.

One time in particular I remember having to go to the dean's office just a few days before graduation.

It was awful going into that office to face her. She

looked up at me with staring eyes, and I wished the building would catch on fire. That would be one way to get out of there.

"So," she said. "You're back again."

She just kept looking at me coldly, and my heart was heavy with the guilt of being undisciplined and rebellious. Her unblinking gaze seemed to say everything: "Why can't you be an obedient student nurse like the others? Why can't you live by the rules? Why do you have to rebel against everyone and everything?"

The sense of failure, of inadequacy, of not measuring up made me hate myself. However, it was a relief that she merely scolded me for being the "ringleader" of a group of girls who thought it would be fun to dump buckets of water in the halls. It was just one more example of my irresponsible behavior, of being "caught up in the moment," and not thinking of the repercussions.

While in high school I had found it daring and even exciting to be around the girls who smoked and read dirty books. Their "wildness" fascinated me. They seemed so unrestrained and free. In nursing school the "wild" girls were even wilder. They defied the rules; they dared getting caught. These girls gathered in Betty's room for all night parties. The danger of being caught at one of them made it even more exciting to go.

One night I'd go to Betty's room for a party, then the next I'd look very pious as I sang in the trio for a church group. I felt torn between the two ways of life.

With tears in her eyes, Sally, our pianist, stopped me in the hall one day.

"Nell," she said, "I need to talk to you."

We went into the cafeteria and got a cup of coffee.

"I don't know where to start," she faltered.

"I think I know," I said. "The girls want to kick me out of the trio. Right?"

Sally burst into tears.

"Oh, Nell", she wept, "it sounds so cruel. But don't you know why, really? You've been backsliding since the day you arrived at school. You get into trouble all the time. You refuse to obey the rules. We have a Christian group, Nell. We carry the name of Jesus Christ, and we represent Him. We can't allow you to bring shame on His name."

I didn't argue with her. As a matter of fact, I agreed with her wholeheartedly. I ruined the group. I was a failure. Who could blame them for not wanting me?

Who needs it anyway? I thought. *I have enough to do to get through school.*

My training consisted of a three-year program, an excellent combination of books and bedside practice. Nurse's training involves learning to *observe*, then learning to *evaluate* what you have observed. A nurse learns to *chart*, to write out observations carefully and accurately.

In spite of myself, I was becoming a nurse, even though I constantly feared facing a situation I couldn't handle.

After six months of intensive classroom training, we were "capped." That ceremony signified the beginning of our actual nursing experience. We went out onto the floors of the hospital and worked with real live people.

Terror!

I don't know how to be a nurse, I moaned to myself. *I'll never learn. I'm such a mess. What if I botch it?* Every morning on the way out to the floor, I stopped at a restroom, my fear causing me to either vomit or have diarrhea.

One day my fears proved to be well-founded. I checked in at the nurse's station where my instructor greeted me.

"Good morning, Miss Collins," she said pleasantly. She handed me some cards. "These are the patients assigned to you this shift. You will want to look the cards over carefully to determine exactly what each person needs done today."

I looked over the cards and saw that some patients were

scheduled for x-ray, and one man needed his hearing tested.

"What are you doing for Mrs. Jones today?" she queried.

I started shaking. "A colostomy irrigation," I whispered. I had never really done one before, I'd only practiced on Herman, the dummy, in the nursing arts lab.

"Might as well do it now," she said.

The instructor went with me to the equipment room. She watched me gather the needed supplies: a metal container for water, some rubber tubing, a clamp, and an ample supply of towels. Taking a deep breath, I placed the articles on a big tray and covered them with a towel. So far so good.

A colostomy is a surgically-made opening in the abdominal wall. This opening is connected to the colon, thereby becoming the rectum, or the passage through which the waste materials leave the body. The colostomy must be cleaned out, or irrigated, on a regular basis. *How did I do the irrigation on the dummy?* I frantically tried to remember.

The correct method of colostomy irrigation is to insert a tube into the opening and unclamp the tube so that water can run through the tube and into the opening. Then the nurse clamps it again, gently removing the tube, having control of it at all times. Sounds easy enough.

We walked into the room.

"Good morning, Mrs. Jones," I said brightly. "I'm going to irrigate your colostomy now." Mrs. Jones looked up, startled. It never occurred to me that it would have been so much better to see her ahead of time to explain the procedure gently, giving her a few minutes to prepare herself emotionally.

She might have wondered why the instructor was with me, but she didn't ask, and I didn't say. She found out soon enough.

Without another word, I took the tube and inserted it into the opening. Then I unclamped the tube so that the water could drain into the opening. The force of the water surprised me; I didn't realize it would come out so fast. I was afraid too much water was going into the opening. In panic I yanked the tube out, forgetting to clamp it, and it flipped up and hit the poor woman in the face. Horrified, I grabbed the tube and held it up so it wouldn't soak the bed.

My instructor never looked at me. She spoke only to Mrs. Jones, who by this time was wailing.

"It's okay, Mrs. Jones," she said softly, "It's okay. We'll take care of all this." She patted Mrs. Jones' arm while I used the towels to blot up the mess I had made. My instructor quickly and efficiently finished the procedure, talking quietly to Mrs. Jones the whole time, comforting her, reassuring her. She said not a word to me.

Afterwards, out in the hallway, she spoke to me sternly. She did not have to tell me I had failed miserably . . . again.

But worse than messing up the procedure was my attitude toward the woman. She had cancer; she was afraid; she was a person with needs. My concern was for me, not her. My desire was to "look good" in front of the supervisor, but I was unconcerned about the patient's deep needs and emotional distress.

One morning I checked my mailbox and in it I found a handwritten note from my supervisor asking me to come to her office for an efficiency evaluation. Though I was accustomed to getting infractions notices, this note panicked me. The routine evaluations were scheduled for much later. Something must be wrong. I wondered if it was related to the colostomy irrigation.

I went directly to her office in the basement of the freshman dorm.

When I saw her, I thought, *That is just what I would like to be.* Neat. Clean. Starched. Professional. Her graying hair was pulled back neatly in a chignon, her horn-rimmed glasses gave her a "strictly business" look. I wished I had that look.

She asked me to come into the room and sit down. She closed the door behind me. Then she started pacing.

"Miss Collins," she finally said, "as you know we evaluate your efficiency on the unit as well as in the classroom. Your classroom efficiency has been fairly stable. But I'm concerned, really *concerned*, about your problems with nursing skills."

I dared not look at her. Biting my lip to keep from crying, I studied the floor. *Oh, no!* My shoes were scuffed and coffee stained my pinafore.

"Your problems, Miss Collins," she continued, "are in two basic areas. The first is your appearance." She gazed at me, from my wrinkled cap to my dirty shoes. "I don't know how to say this, Miss Collins, but we insist that our nurses maintain a standard of neatness. When a nurse's personal appearance is slovenly, then it gives the impression that we are slipshod in the care we take of patients. Do you understand what I am saying, Miss Collins?"

I nodded, tears blinding me. *My life is out of control,* I screamed in my mind. *I can't control myself. I eat too much and look like a slob.*

"The second area, Miss Collins," she continued, "is your charting. Look at this notation you made on Mr. Zebrouski in 405. 'Patient's OK.' Really, Miss Collins; 'Patient's OK' does not communicate anything. We know he's alive, but you have given us no information about his condition. Is he in bed or in a chair? How is his color? His breathing? His frame of mind? Does he have any complaints? If he's on oxygen, how much? Does he have a catheter? Is it draining? How much is it draining, and what does the drainage look like? Do you see what I mean?" I nodded miserably.

"Miss Collins," she said, softer, gentler now. "Being a good nurse involves many things, but above all we must remember that the patient is a *person*. It's a big change to go from the dummy we use in the classroom to real people. Every patient is somebody's husband or wife or child, one who is loved, one who has plans and hopes which temporarily have been interrupted by medical problems. Our job is to get that person back to his 'other life' in the most efficient and orderly manner possible. Do you see the importance of what I'm saying?"

I nodded again, unable to speak. I dragged out of her office, my heart heavy with grief.

What is wrong with me? Everybody else seems to have it together, but not me. Not me. Life is so meaningless. It takes so much energy just to get through the day. I thought that nursing was the answer for me, but I'm not even a good nurse.

In spite of my many failures at "having it together" and my lack of self-confidence, I worked hard to improve. I must have done some things right, because graduation day finally came, and I, proud but nervous, officially graduated and soon after that passed my state board of health examinations and became a "R.N."

After graduation, my life changed very little from when I was in school. For the first few months, another nurse and I lived in an apartment house close to the hospital and worked nights in the pediatric unit, or "peds," as we called it.

"Peds" meant babies, sick babies under two years old. The big room held twelve cribs, each with an equipment table next to it. In one small section at the side was the nurse's station with all the charts and office materials.

Many of the babies needed cleft palate surgery. These babies were born with a hole in the roof of the mouth and could not swallow properly. A baby with a cleft palate had to be fed with a gavage tube which would get the formula into his throat, bypassing the cleft palate. Other babies were there for hernia surgery or repairs on congenital hip deformities.

The parents of these babies usually had gone home by the time I got to work. An aide and I changed diapers and fed babies for eight continuous hours. Sometimes the boredom seemed intolerable.

Occasionally, the monotony was broken by an emergency situation, and it was exhilarating when we managed to save a baby's life. In those instances, I gave all the credit to the wonders of medical science. But sometimes, in spite of our best efforts, the baby died. In those situations I blamed God. *How could He do a thing like that?* I brooded.

One night an aide and I were working. Six babies needed to be gavaged and I was running late on the feeding schedule. I was tired, irritable. The aide had been changing diapers and taking temperatures.

"Miss Collins," she said, "Timmy's temp is 103 degrees. You'd better call the doctor."

"I'll take care of it," I snapped. *Who does she think she is, telling me to call the doctor?* I hurriedly finished feeding Bobby, carefully putting the crib rail up. I went over to Timmy's crib and took his temperature again. Sure enough, it was 103°, right on the dot.

As I went to the telephone to call the doctor, I thought, *Why did I ever think it would be so great to be a nurse? How did I wind up at three o'clock in the morning with twelve wet, fussy babies? Life surely has more meaning than this.*

On the next Saturday I got off work at 7:30 a.m., went to the bus station, and took the first bus home.

Had my folks been right after all? Perhaps the key to being happy was to work for God. Could my misery be the result of not "doing enough" for Him? "The world's" way was shallow and empty. The only thing left was to try religion again.

My only goal by this time was to find peace. *No matter what,* I had to find peace for my troubled heart.

My mind was made up to go someplace far away and be a missionary-nurse, after all. *If that's what it takes to make God happy, then I'll do it.*

I had to do something.

On the bus on the way home I thought how happy it would make Mom. At last I would fulfill her long-standing dream that I would serve God on a mission station.

Daddy picked me up at the bus station and hardly said a word on the way home. As soon as I got my suitcase into the house, he went for a long walk. Things had not changed much at home.

Mom was working in the kitchen. "Hey, Mom," I said, "you're not going to believe this . . ." Before I could finish, my brother roared into the room, looking for something to eat. He had grown so tall! Then it occurred to me that he was almost eighteen, and boys were being drafted to go to Viet Nam. He had grown up, and I didn't even know him. He said something about a "big date," and he was off again.

Mom said, "It's been a long time since you've been home, Nelia Anne. Is something wrong?"

"No, Mom, not wrong. I think things may be right. You see, I want to serve the Lord. I want to go to a home mission field and be a missionary nurse."

Mom beamed proudly. *For once,* I thought, *maybe I can do something right for her. I have disappointed her so often.*

While in nursing school, my visits home had been few, and I had not shared with Mom my inner frustrations and conflicts about God. If she had had any idea how confused I was, she would have been so disappointed in me. It was best, I decided, to just try to work through the confusion in my life by myself.

On the application papers Mom gave me, there was a place to write out my "testimony."

They won't let me go, I thought, *if I don't use the right words.* Of course I knew that Jesus had died for the sins of the world, and I explained it very clearly on the application blank. The problem was that I did not realize then that Jesus had died for the sins of Nell Collins.

And it was on that basis that I went to a home mission field to do "missionary" nursing.

V

The mission headquarters assigned me to a small hospital in a western state. Images of cowboys and tumbleweeds filled my brain with excitement. *My first trip out of Indiana! And no parents, supervisors, or chaperones to keep an eye on me.*

A nurse from the hospital was also going West, so she and another friend decided to ride out with me, as far as the mission station. As we crammed my 1954 Chevy with clothes, radios, and popcorn poppers, we laughed with high-pitched jubilance.

By the time we reached Oklahoma City, the pioneer spirit swelled. Traveling across country on Route 66 we squealed with glee when we saw the oil wells and red dirt.

Soon desert wasteland surrounded us. As the other gals chatted about their plans, I thought about my life in the West, and the thrill paled a bit. I wondered, *What will it be like, living in a mission hospital? I hope I'm doing the right thing. It'll be worth it, if only I can be happy . . . Oh, well. At least I'm doing something halfway exciting for a change.*

My mission hospital served a little town not far from the Mexican border. As I pulled off the four-lane highway and onto the narrow road into town, I noticed the landscape. For miles upon miles the grey desert stretched, broken only occasionally by clumps of straggling, water-starved weeds. Here and there a cactus plant defied the scorching sun, and a yucca pierced the sky with its rigid spines.

So different, I thought, *from the lush green of Indiana. Wonder if I'll miss the leaves changing color in autumn?*

The hot wind lashed at my face through the open car window. When I stopped at an intersection, the heat broiled up from the pavement. Perspiration rolled into my eyes and my wet shirt clung to my back. In the distance a range of mountains broke the monotony of the flat desert wasteland, and the purplish blue above the mountainous horizon promised cooler temperatures in the hills.

The mission headquarters had warned me that many of the villagers suffered intense poverty, so the beautiful homes edging the town surprised me. *Not everybody is poor*, I thought. The architects had used adobe in these lavish homes, but only for effect. They trimmed the buildings and fences in decorative wrought iron, resulting in stylish western ranch homes with a Spanish flair.

Closer to town the poverty became more apparent. Scrubby, dark-skinned boys, barefoot and shirtless, ran along the street, shiny black hair standing straw-like atop their heads. A swarthy-looking man in old jeans, a dirty white T-shirt, and high-heeled cowboy boots swaggered along the main street. He wandered into a greasy spoon with no name except "EAT."

The printed directions took me easily to the hospital, a one-story yellow brick building. Built originally in a square configuration, it now sprawled shapelessly because of the various wings added over the years.

The hospital administrator greeted me warmly and took me on a quick tour of the hospital.

"Our hospital," he said, "is small but quite functional. We have an area for surgery and a small emergency room. We have a number of babies delivered every day, so the Ob-Gyn unit is one of our busiest places."

The hospital seemed so tiny compared to the huge metropolitan hospital where I had worked in Indiana.

"Your assignment," he said, "will be pediatrics." He introduced me to the Pediatric Supervisor for whom I would be working.

More crying babies! I thought. On my application paper I had given my area of experience as pediatrics, but I secretly had hoped my assignment would be something quite different, because I was tired of sick babies.

On the one hand I felt that the way to happiness was to work for the Lord, yet on the other hand I was sure that serving God meant doing things I didn't want to do and giving up all earthly pleasure for Him. I guessed I could "sacrifice" my desire for a change of assignment and work in peds again.

We walked next door to the nurse's dorm, a building with about twenty rooms. *This place looks just like my room at school*, I thought. *Even has that shiny paint.*

Some of the rooms, I noticed, were all fixed up with pictures on the walls, plants, knickknacks, and even rugs on the floor. The people who lived in those rooms evidently were committed to spending the rest of their lives at that place. No way was I going to get *that* settled. I determined to keep the room stoic and unadorned, so everyone would know I was suffering for the Lord. Besides, I enjoyed being a slob. *If I fix it up,* I thought, *I'll have to worry about dumb old doilies and all that stuff. I'll just put my clothes in the closet and concentrate on serving God.* I also secretly thought that dowdiness was a way to gain points with the Lord, so I decided to avoid anything stylish.

As I began to know the other nurses I found that here, too, they seemed to be divided into two groups, the "goody-goodies" and the "not-so-goodies." Some of them, of course, had been there a hundred years and they *never* did anything wrong, but some of the younger girls were secret swingers. Again, I felt out of it; I didn't fit in anywhere or with anyone. Most of the nurses were friendly to me, but with some of them I felt that our friendship was highly conditional. They would like me *if* my appearance, my behavior, my personality met their approval. Otherwise, forget it. Often I felt on trial, that I was being judged. My little room seemed as empty and friendless as the houses I had lived in as a child.

Juanita, a Spanish aide at the hospital, worked in pediatrics with me. She was the only person there who made me feel at ease. She accepted me just as I was. Her talk was a little rough, sometimes even harsh, but I knew she cared about me.

One day she stopped me in the hall and shook her head at me until her black hair bounced. "Nellie, Nellie," she said. "Why didn't you press that uniform? It looks terrible." Her bluntness didn't offend me, because I knew that what she thought she would say to my face, not behind my back as so many others did.

In the same breath she added in her thick Spanish accent, "Nellie, you must come to my house for dinner tonight. You get sick and tired of hospital food. Tonight we have tacos and burritos and stuff ourselves good, eh?" She winked and laughed as she rambled down the corridor. Juanita liked to eat as much as I did.

Juanita lived in a simple bungalow with her husband and four children. The children, all under six years old, hung onto Juanita's skirt and looked around her with big eyes at the stranger who had come to dinner. Within minutes, however, they were climbing all over me and I was down on the floor giving horsey rides. Soon I was babysitting for Juanita's children regularly, and I began to feel like a member of the family.

Juanita gave me real emotional support. She was unaffected and unsophisticated, but her love for me was genuine. With regard to religion, the outer trappings in

Juanita's home were the same as I had known as a child. Juanita and her family went to church and talked about the Lord. But a *peace* prevailed in her home, a freedom from tension, a lack of strife. I couldn't pinpoint what made the difference; I just knew it felt *good* to be there.

At the hospital, most of the children on the ward stayed only a few days following surgery or other treatment. However, Ricardo's hospitalization lasted months, until he was considered an almost permanent patient. He became another good friend to me. An eleven-year-old boy with multiple sclerosis, he had been unable to escape when his house had caught fire. Severe burns covered most of his body.

One day, as I pushed him in his wheelchair down to physical therapy for a water bath, he seemed depressed. Quiet. His dark eyes usually twinkled with good humor, but not today.

"Que pasa?" I asked him. "What's the matter?" Ricardo had become my unofficial teacher of Spanish. We spent much time together, and both of us enjoyed his teaching me Spanish words and phrases. I hoped that by speaking Spanish I might lift his spirits.

"Nada," he said, "nothing." He dropped his head, and my heart ached for him. How I wanted to help this little boy! I took him downstairs to the sunroom and got us each a Coke. He stared out the window for a long, long time.

"Nellie," when he said my name it sounded like *Nallie*, "you know I have prayed and prayed that God would make me well, but it still hurts. It hurts so bad. Why won't God take away the hurt?"

I turned my face so he wouldn't see the tears in my eyes. "I don't know, Ricardo. I really don't."

His poor little body, twisted in the wheelchair, looked scarred and helpless. How *could* God refuse to take away his hurt?

As the months passed I grew more and more frustrated with my inability to do anything that made a real difference. The sickness and poverty and ignorance of many of the people appalled me. Doris, the public health nurse, sometimes invited me to go visiting with her. One day we went up into the mountains to call on a family with a sick baby.

"Now brace yourself," she told me. "Some of these families live in really wretched conditions."

We climbed in her four-speed Volkswagen bug and headed up the twisting mountain trail. Doris had scrawled crude directions on the back of an envelope: "Cross over the arroyo, go to the old Johnson place, follow the trail to the fork, then go two more miles." Doris knew her way around the hills.

Finally we found the Hermonos' one-room adobe shack. On the rickety porch, a bloody-looking deer hung by the hind legs, and flies swarmed around it.

The mother sat on the dirt floor inside the shack with a screaming baby in her arms. Five or six other little ones ran around, and one stretched out on a mat on the floor. The mats appeared to be all they had for beds.

Doris examined the baby. He was becoming dehydrated from having diarrhea, and the diaper area flamed red and raw. No wonder the poor thing screamed. We cleaned him up and then applied the medication the doctor had sent for the rash.

"The diarrhea must be stopped," Doris said firmly, "and you must get him to drink liquids. Do you know how to make Jello water?" The mother eyed us suspiciously as she shook her head.

Doris showed her exactly what to do and explained how to take care of the rash. "Keep him on a clean blanket, and leave the diapers off. It needs air to heal."

After a few more instructions, Doris said, "If he isn't

better tomorrow, you must take him to the hospital. Do you have a way to get him there?"

She nodded, but she looked both wary and defiant. We doubted if she would follow our instructions, but we had done all we could.

We went back down the mountain with a sense of futility. Too many people lived in poverty and ignorance and filth. What we were doing did not seem to be making a difference at all.

Another day, on my way to work at six o'clock in the morning, I saw a car pull into the emergency entrance. A woman in the back seat was screaming. Her face contorted in pain; she writhed hysterically. Another nurse heard the commotion, and we both ran to the car as it screeched to a halt.

The man driving the car mopped his dripping face on his shirtsleeve as he quickly told us the grim story. He and his wife had left the mountain an hour before, and on the way she realized the baby was coming. She had tried to delay the delivery by keeping the baby from passing through the birth canal.

The other nurse and I climbed into the back seat and finished the delivery. The baby was dead.

My heart was heavy, and a sense of futility and hopelessness pervaded me. Spiritually, I felt as dead as that stillborn baby. The world was so full of trouble and heartache. *If there is a God*, I thought glumly, *He must be cruel to let people suffer so*. It all seemed like such a waste.

I went to see Juanita that night and she cried when I told her about the baby.

"Poor, dead baby," she wept. "Poor, poor Mama."

"I just don't get it, Juanita," I said. "Why do people have to go through all of this? All I see is pain and hurt and death. I'm beginning to think that God doesn't even exist. If He did, He'd take care of things a little better."

In her quiet, supportive way, Juanita let me spew and sputter. Then she simply said, "Nellie, you just have to trust Him."

"*Trust* Him?" I said bitterly. "How can anybody trust a God that doesn't care?"

During that period of time, frustration and resentment churned inside of me. I began to feel nauseated, then finally I began vomiting blood. I had a bleeding ulcer, and one of the doctors put me on a "sippy" diet consisting of mostly milk and oatmeal. For a few months I couldn't eat tacos or any other hot Mexican foods.

My frustration expressed itself in my old habit pattern of rebelliousness. I did all kinds of loud and ridiculous things to get attention. I even put taps on my nursing shoes so people could hear me clicking up and down the hallways.

One night several of us drove from the hospital to a root beer stand in a nearby town. It was a favorite hangout of the local young people, and as usual, a bunch of boys were there. They came over to our table and we all laughed and joked, then we divided up and drove both cars back to the hospital. I rode in the car with Jack. He walked with me to the dorm.

"What's a missionary do for fun?" he asked bluntly. I gathered he was interested in having a good time.

"Whatever she feels like," I answered, just as bluntly, looking him straight in the eye. "All I care about is having fun. Life is full of miserable people, and I don't intend to be one of them."

Jack told me about a Mexican street party he was going to later that night.

"The action starts about midnight," he said, "D'ya wanna go?"

"Well," I said, hesitating. "We have hours, you know. The doors are locked at ten." Then I had a wild idea. "But I could climb out my window. They'd never miss me."

"Whattya know," Jack said with a smirk, "a swinging missionary. I'll be at the end of the driveway at a quarter to twelve."

Glancing at the clock in our small lobby, I noticed that it was nearly ten o'clock already. *Just enough time to shower and change*, I thought.

After my shower, I made a big production of yawning and saying goodnight to everyone. I closed my door and locked it.

My first purchase out there had been a pair of cowboy boots and a cowboy hat. *That's what I'll wear*, I thought. *Jeans, sweatshirt, boots and hat*. I grabbed my baritone ukelele, thinking it might be fun to take to the party.

At eleven-forty exactly I turned off the light. I quietly removed the screen from my window, then propped it against the wall in my room. With some effort I pulled myself onto the ledge, then jumped, dropping heavily behind the shrubbery. I spotted Jack and his "wheels" at the end of the driveway.

A few miles away, an entire street had been barricaded and people thronged into the street laughing gaily. Four men on a little platform played and sang loud Mexican music. Bright lights illuminated the brilliant colors of their wildly decorated sombreros. Young Mexican girls dressed in full skirts and peasant blouses whirled to the music. When the band took a break I got out my uke and led a group in singing Spanish folk songs. For a few hours, I tried to forget my misery and lose my feelings of emptiness in the festive atmosphere. We partied until dawn, then I slipped back through my window and replaced the screen. No problem whatsoever. Once again I felt torn between two worlds. Jack and his crowd promised excitement and adventure, the Christian people in my life promised stability and respect. I became a chameleon, changing colors to blend with the situation.

A day or two later I bumped into one of the other

nurses in the hallway. This nurse always seemed to be excited about the Lord, and on this day she had a letter in her hand, and she was beaming.

"Oh, Nellie," she said, "I got a letter from my brother this morning and he has come to know the Lord. Isn't that wonderful?"

I nodded and said, "Oh, yeah, that's just great." I didn't know what she was so excited about, but I didn't want her to think I didn't understand. It was just one more example of the game I played.

One night I was sneaking out to go to another party with Jack. He had a friend visiting him who needed a date, so I tried to convince one of the other nurses to sneak out with me, but she wouldn't do it. That didn't stop me from being an "evangelist" of sorts. I had become a one-woman crusade, and my goal was to persuade everyone to join me in looking for the pleasures of today. The more intense my efforts were to have a "good time," the more miserable I became.

Deeply dissatisfied with myself and everyone else, I had grown resentful of religion, God, and the do-gooders who made me look bad by comparison. They all made me sick.

Christianity is a farce, I concluded. *What a waste! Christians are all a bunch of phonies. It sounds good, but it doesn't mean a thing. They can have their God. If anybody tries to tell ME about God, I'm gonna hit 'em in the face.*

I was finished, *finished* with God. Over 20 years of my life had been wasted trying to be religious, trying to please other people. *I'm not gonna do it any more,* I fumed. *I've had it!*

Having been at the mission barely a year, I packed it all up and came back to Indiana, breaking both my two-year contract and my mother's heart.

So what? I thought. *She'll get over it. Who cares, anyway?*

It was not long before I was once again working pediatrics at night in a hospital in Indiana. This time I worked in the isolation ward rather than the nursery. I hated my job. I hated being a nurse. I hated myself.

I wanted to die.

That's it, I thought. *I'll kill myself and put an end to this misery. It's the only way. I'm not gonna mess around with pills. I'll just get a gun and shoot myself. But where do people buy guns? I'm too dumb even to know how to get my hands on a gun. I'm not even smart enough to kill myself.*

Joan, a girl at the hospital, tried to bring me out of my depression, but I resented her for her quiet spirit and sweet way. She irritated me because she seemed to have it "all together."

Goody two-shoes, I thought sourly. *Always so cheerful and optimistic. Little Miss Pollyanna herself.*

No matter how nasty I was, however, she remained kind and thoughtful to me, and her constancy of caring impressed me. She never said much to me, but when I would growl and complain about some hospital problem, she said, "That must be hard. I'll be praying for you."

I ignored her. All I wanted was to find a gun.

I never verbalized my agony to a living soul. If I had talked openly with anybody, it might have been possible for someone to have helped me. But no one knew how miserable I was. They saw only a cold, aloof nurse with an "I don't care" attitude.

VI

Working the night shift meant trying to catch up on sleep during the day. Being so depressed, I found myself unable to sleep or adjust to the honking of horns and the chattering of pedestrians outside my window.

One afternoon I rolled out of bed, exhausted. For hours I had lain there, tortured by the terrible need for sleep and plagued by the total inability to slip into that blessed state of restfulness.

Dragging myself over to the window, I raised the shade. The bright sunlight hurt my eyes; I quickly pulled it down again. As I passed my mirror, a hollow-eyed specter stared back at me, and I wondered, *How can a nurse look so terrible?*

Flipping on the radio, I heard the plaintive song lyric, "What's it all about, Alfie?"

What IS it all about? I thought. *It's going to work, going to bed, getting up, going to work, until one of these days you get up enough nerve to shoot yourself. That's what it's all about, Alfie.*

I got into the shower and turned it on, really hot. The scalding water hurt, but I didn't care. Nothing mattered anymore.

Where's that uniform I wore yesterday? I wondered. *Just hope I didn't drip spaghetti sauce on it last night.* The overstuffed chair was heaped with clothes and books, and the dresser had mounds of junk piled on it, but I located the uniform and pulled it on over my embarrassingly full figure and massive "spare tire."

In the kitchen, hardly an inch of countertop showed through the stacks of dishes. Taking the lid off the old percolator I whiffed the rancid coffee from another day's brew. *Oh, well,* I thought. *I'll just stop by Dunkin' Donuts on the way downtown.*

Wouldn't my mother have a fit if she saw this mess? I thought. *Oh, well. Who cares, anyway?*

By sheer force of will I dragged myself out of the apartment and to the hospital. Two other nurses on duty during my shift were already there when I got off the elevator, but they didn't see me. I went down the hall to get a drink of water, and as I got closer to the nurse's station, I overheard them talking.

"Guess who's late again. Nasty Nell," one said.

"It figures. She's a zombie half the time and the rest she just spews venom. Sure would like to see her transferred to another shift. Another ward. Another *planet.*"

They both snickered.

"Wonder what her problem is? I've never seen anybody such a mess."

Quietly I slipped into the restroom before they had a chance to see me. I went into one of the stalls and cried as noiselessly as possible. The rotten thing about it was that they were so *right.*

Composing myself with great effort, I walked back out to the nurse's station. A chill fell over the little group, and no one spoke. Silently I went into the isolation ward. Grabbing a clean apron and mask, I prepared to check the first patient.

The isolation wing of the floor was designed to care for children with contagious diseases. Each child had a little cubicle, glassed in all around. Inside each cubicle was a crib with tall side bars and a bedside table for supplies.

The little boy in the first cubicle, just seven years old,

was dying with spinal meningitis. He had been under treatment for several days, but the type of meningitis he had was nearly always fatal. He was heavily sedated. His mother waved to me from the hallway, indicating she wanted to talk to me. I took off the apron and mask and threw them in the barrel to be sterilized, and I washed my hands thoroughly at the sink. We had to be fastidious in isolation to keep from spreading diseases.

"Can you tell me . . ." the mother said, faltering, "what I mean is . . . well, can you tell me what is happening with my child? No one is telling me anything other than he has meningitis and you're doing all you can."

She looked haggard and distraught. Days and nights of worried sleeplessness showed in the dark circles under her eyes.

What could I say to the poor woman? Her boy was dying, and we could not do one thing to save him. *But if she doesn't know,* I thought, *I'm sure not going to be the one to tell her. No, sir. Somebody else can do that little number.*

"Well, he's sleeping now," I said lamely. *You dope!* I thought to myself, *Any idiot can see he's asleep.*

"What I mean is, is he going to get well? Can you give me any hope?"

Hope! I thought despairingly. *Lady, there is no hope. Not for this life and not for eternity. It is all a hopeless, meaningless mess.* But I said to her, "Maybe you can talk with the doctor tomorrow."

I saw her back straighten ever so slightly, and a look of confidence came into her eyes. "You are doing everything you can. I realize that," she said softly. "I just have to leave him in the hands of Jesus. I *know* I can trust Him."

I changed the subject quickly. "Why don't you go to the lounge and have a cup of coffee? Maybe that would make you feel better."

As she turned and walked away, my heart seethed with bitterness. *Jesus? What does He have to do with this?* But I envied the serenity I saw in her face.

A few nights later I got a call from Mark, a fellow who had dated a friend of mine while we were in nursing school. He had heard of my return to Indiana and asked if I would like to go out for a Coke the next afternoon. He worked nights in a factory, so his free time coincided with mine.

Good ol' Mark, I thought. *The fun-loving, party boy of all time.* His lack of good looks did not slow him down one bit. He drove a fast car and lived a daring and rakish lifestyle. *A lot like me,* I thought. *We'll get along just fine. Maybe he can lift my spirits.*

Mark and I began to see each other regularly. At first I thought that having this new man in my life would make me happy, but the relationship disappointed me. He intended to have a good time, regardless of the consequences or the people in his way. His selfishness irritated me; I wanted him to make *me* happy, to be my prince charming, to make my world a place of bliss.

All I wanted was to find peace or happiness or *something*. That *something* eluded me. What could it be? There did not seem to be any answers, regardless of where I looked. Nothing, absolutely nothing, satisfied my heart.

My attitude became nastier and more sullen every day. When I went out with Mark, however, I tried to appear cheerful, knowing he would never tolerate a snarling, disagreeable date.

One evening he picked me up at home to have supper before going to work. It had been another one of those miserable, sleepless days. I had wrestled with insomnia for hours, and I struggled out of bed.

Mark honked his car horn for me and I dragged myself outside. My eyes, tired and red from lack of sleep, glared at him in his stupid car. Morosely I sagged into the car seat and slammed the door behind me.

"What's your beef?" Mark asked sharply.

"Nothing." I stared through the windshield.

"Come on, now. What's wrong?"

"Nothing. I don't know. Leave me alone." I started crying.

"Oh brother. I don't need this. I don't have to put up with a bawling broad." He turned around and drove back to my apartment. "Get out, and turn your tears on someone else."

Standing on the steps, I watched him roar down the street, squealing his tires as he turned the corner. I had hoped to find happiness through a close human relationship, and that hadn't worked either.

Where can I get a gun? I thought. *It's the only answer. I'm a no-good mess.*

With no place else to go, I figured I might as well drive on down to work.

As I neared the hospital, I noticed the "toughness" of the neighborhood, the reek of inner-city blight. Every day people were beaten or robbed or murdered in this area. I didn't care. I didn't even lock my doors. *Maybe somebody will pull the trigger for me,* I thought dismally. *Save me the trouble.*

On a street corner I saw a pawn shop. It was barricaded for the night, but I thought, *Bet they have guns in there.*

I parked two or three blocks from the hospital, almost daring somebody to slip out of an alley and slit my throat. I was actually disappointed to have made it to the hospital without getting murdered.

A day or two later Mark called me and acted as though nothing had happened. We resumed dating, but I tried to hide my misery from him.

At work Joan broke down my defenses by just being nice to me. She introduced me to her roommate. She was also a Christian and a nurse. Joan and her roommate both had those qualities of stability and peacefulness that I so desperately wanted.

One night Joan asked me if I could give her a ride home from work. *Why not?* I thought. *It's on the way.*

[*58*]

Hungry after work, we pulled into a 24-hour drive-in restaurant and I ordered two large Cokes and two large fries through the metal speaker attached to the post by the car. We chatted casually about hospital problems and routines until the car-hop brought our order.

"Some breakfast," the car-hop muttered under her breath, not realizing that we had worked all night. "Oh, well. Takes all kinds."

Joan smiled at the car-hop, then turned to me. She asked, "How's everything going, Nell?"

For a few minutes I didn't answer. I was afraid to start talking for fear I wouldn't be able to stop. But something about Joan let me know that I could trust her. I poured out my angry and miserable heart to her.

Joan sipped her Coke and looked at me. Her french fries were getting cold.

"Nell," she said, "there's something I've been wanting to talk with you about. Please don't get mad at me, but I need to ask you something really important."

She spoke softly and quickly, as though she had to speak her mind before losing the courage to do so.

"I know that you are in real distress, Nell," she said. "Your unhappiness is apparent to everyone who knows you. I'm just wondering if you understand that Jesus Christ can meet the deepest needs of your heart."

I swallowed hard.

Part of me started to respond in anger; another part of me felt like I was drowning and someone was trying to grab hold of my hand before I went under for the final time.

"I know that you used to work in a mission hospital, Nell," she continued. "And I know that you were raised in a religious home. But, Nell, knowing God in a personal way is something that happens in the *heart*."

As Joan talked, it all began making sense to me. It was as though I had been hiding in a dark room all my life, and now someone was showing me the way to the light.

She talked a long time about God's goodness, and how it was man's sin and rebellion that caused our world to be under a curse, a curse of disease, deterioration, and death. I had heard all my life about Adam and Eve's disobedience in the Garden of Eden, but I began to see that because of God's perfection and holiness *sin* had caused a great barrier between God and the people on the cursed planet.

"People all over the world," Joan said, "try to find God by being religious or by doing good things, but it's never enough. Religion can't remove that barrier of sin. That's why Christ had to come to earth and die for my sin and for yours."

We kept talking as I drove Joan to her apartment. What she said made sense. All my life I had thought that God would accept me if I could just, somehow, be good enough. But I failed to live up to His standards.

"All you need to do, Nell," Joan was saying, "is open your heart to Jesus and accept what He has already done for you."

Could it be true? Could it really be that simple?

"Do you know what it means, Nell? If you receive Him into your heart, He will make you *a new creature!* When you truly accept Jesus as your very own Savior, then He comes into your life. You are completely and perfectly wrapped in His righteousness. All of your sins and even all of your failures are gone forever. He says, 'Come unto Me all ye who are weary and heavy-laden, and I will give you rest.' "

Rest! My hands began trembling, and I was afraid I would cry. I couldn't make a sound. How I wanted *rest*.

Could I actually believe it? That Jesus had already paid for my sin? That there was nothing I could do to make myself good enough for God? That Christ had come to earth and died to pay the penalty for my sin? That all I had to do was respond to Him and accept, by faith, what He had already done? That He wanted to change me, to make me a new creation? How I wanted to believe it was true!

I did not receive Christ as my Savior that night, but I did make a decision to be willing to understand more about Him.

"Thanks, Joan," I said as she got out of the car. "Really, *thanks*."

The next time I saw Mark I tried to tell him about my conversation with Joan.

"Wait a minute," he said. "You're not gonna go and get religious on me, are you? Why would you want to go and spoil a good thing?"

Quickly I changed the subject, determining to steer away from anything that would cause a problem between us. We agreed to go out for a Coke the next day.

Later that summer, Joan and her roommate asked me to share their apartment, and I accepted without reservation. An elderly lady had converted the entire second floor of her big old house into a three-bedroom apartment. The other two girls worked different hours than I did, so we saw each other infrequently, but I noticed the same quality in these girls that I had seen in Sally Williams at school and in Juanita at the mission hospital. I couldn't define it or understand it. They weren't perfect; they had faults. But what they possessed was a deep peace, a confidence, a serenity that I desperately wanted.

On October 8, 1965, I came home from work in the early morning, as usual. The other girls were gone and I had the whole place to myself. I rummaged through the refrigerator and ate everything I could find. After "pigging out" on a half gallon of ice cream and a box of Ding Dongs, I felt miserable.

Maybe a nice hot bath will make me feel better, I thought, but as I soaked in the tub I became even more depressed.

After my bath I wrapped myself in a warm robe, and went into the living room, looking for something to read.

A Christian magazine was on the coffee table and I absentmindedly began flipping through it. A brief article titled "Tell Me Again" caught my attention. The story told of a little old toothless man who walked over three mountains to get to the missionary's house. He said:

"You know that man you told me about? The man who died for my sin? What did you say His name was? Tell me again."

I felt just like that little man who had walked over the mountains to hear, just one more time, about Jesus. I didn't see myself as the missionary. I was the person in need of the Savior, and finally I understood who He was and exactly what He had done for me. My whole life had been spent trying to *do* something for God, but now I saw that nothing I could do could take away my sin. Only God could reach down in love to me and provide the Way to Himself. Because of His great love for me, my heart was filled with repentance. I was sorry for my sin, and I wanted Him to change me.

I went back to my mirrored vanity and started rolling my hair in big pink rollers, but the words of the magazine article continued to pierce my heart. I knew that just like the little old toothless man, my search was over. God had found me. I left the vanity and dropped to my knees beside my bed.

"Dear God," I wept and prayed, "I am so sorry for my sin, but now I realize you died for *me*. You paid for my sin by dying on the cross. Come into my heart now and be my Savior. Thank you, Jesus, thank you." I opened my heart and received God's wonderful gift of salvation. What a relief it was to know that I didn't have to earn God's favor. All the religious activity of my life had never brought this kind of peace to my heart.

For the first time in months I crawled into bed and went

to sleep like a baby being rocked in her mother's arms. Insomnia did not plague me; I slept without waking until my alarm sounded.

Upon awakening, my first thought turned to Jesus and what He had done for me. *Thank you, Lord.* I had a deep sense of knowing that what had happened was real, and all I could think about was sharing with others how they, too, could have this wonderful peace. *Mark!* I thought, *I've got to tell Mark!*

A day or two later, Mark came by for me, and we went to the drive-in restaurant for our usual supper of a double burger in a basket with french fries and cole slaw. I didn't know how to tell him, but I wanted him to know what had happened.

He cut me off in mid-sentence.

"Hey, listen. If you want to go off on some religious kick, that's fine. If it's what you want, then it's okay for you. But I'm not interested in that stuff. Period. Don't bore me with it."

My heart sank. I had hoped that Mark and I might marry someday, but, ironically, he was as antagonistic toward God as I had been, and we were growing farther apart each day. Still, I hung onto him, hoping he would change his mind.

The next weekend I went home to tell Mom.

"Why Nelia Anne," she said, a hurt look on her face. "What on earth are you talking about? You accepted the Lord when you were seven years old, under my ministry." She abruptly got up and started digging through some old books.

"Here it is," she said triumphantly. She brought out a dog-eared photograph of a church. On the back was written: "Nelia Anne asked Jesus to be her Savior in this church, 1948."

"Oh, Mom," I said. "I can remember walking down the aisle lots of times. They gave me words to say, and I parroted them. I said the words because I wanted to be pleasing to you and Daddy and God. I wanted God to accept me because I did all those things for Him. It was all ritual, Mom. Can't you see the difference?"

Mom looked at me with a bewildered expression on her face. She looked as though I had stabbed her.

My roommates, however, were thrilled for me. I started going to church with them, and I followed the Lord in believer's baptism. I grabbed every opportunity to hear the Word and be with other Christians. I felt like a starving child who had gone too long without nourishment.

Later I started attending a prayer circle that met once a week in the evening of my day off to pray for the needs of North Africa. We prayed for specific missionaries there. I felt I knew several of them very well, even though they were far away. As we prayed for the needs of the missionaries, I became more and more interested in the Moslem people. As I learned how they go through the rituals of worship, praying five times a day at specific times and in certain ways, I realized that I had been just like those people: religious, yes, but lost. I thought about the women in that culture, trapped in servitude and fear, and I wanted them to know the wonderful freedom found only in Christ.

My good friend Sally Williams from school was now a missionary in Central Africa. It seemed that everyone I knew was doing great things for God in Africa.

The glamour of North Africa intrigued me—even the names in the area: Morocco, Tangier, Casablanca, Algiers, Tunis—echoed with mystery and excitement. I was especially drawn to Algeria and its unique culture. I learned that Algeria is the home of the Tuareg nomads, known for the unusual custom (among Moslems) of men, rather than women, covering their faces with veils. The more I thought about it, the more entranced I became with the idea of serving in Africa.

My hospital experience had been limited to pediatrics, so I knew that I needed to gain some skill in working with adults, since in North Africa I'd probably work with people of all ages. I also needed some courses in Bible college.

Without delay I applied for a transfer to another hospital in the city. Working with adults was one goal, but I also wanted a new beginning, a clean start.

In my work, I felt a sense of utter failure. My rude and angry behavior as a nurse in those days of terrible depression embarrassed me. I wanted to start over where people did not know me before my salvation.

Every detail worked out flawlessly. My application was accepted at a fine hospital in the city; they called me for an interview; they hired me for a staff nurse position in a medical constant care unit. I was able to get a day shift so that I could take Bible college classes in the evenings. I knew it would take three or four years to prepare for Africa, but it would be worth it.

At one of our prayer meetings shortly after this time, a rather remarkable thing happened that I didn't even consider important at the time.

A nurse friend asked me if I might go see a girl named Dottie, who was depressed and threatening to overdose on pills. Dottie lived in a trailer in a rough section of town. As I pulled into the trailer park, I saw trash and junk cars everywhere. Most of the trailers were old, beat-up, and rusty.

It took a long time for Dottie to answer my knock. She reeled and staggered to the door, and looked at me with wild eyes.

"Hi. I'm Nell," I ventured.

I told her that her friend had asked me to stop by. She hesitated a moment, then opened the door and stepped aside.

The filth inside the trailer gagged me. My apartment

was a mess, but this was unbelievable. Flies buzzed around dirty dishes. Beer cans and liquor bottles littered the floor. I suspected that she was on drugs as well as alcohol.

As I looked at the wreckage of this woman's life, I thought, *There but for the grace of God go I. If I'd kept on the way I was headed, this could have been me.*

Since I was on my way to the prayer meeting that night, I gave her the telephone number there and said, "If you get to feeling like you just can't handle it, call me. Don't do anything to hurt yourself without calling me first."

The telephone rang at the prayer meeting. Dottie was on the line, and she was hysterical.

"I've got pills!" she screamed, "and I'm going to take them all!"

With a calm voice I talked and talked; I let her talk; I prayed for her. For an hour we worked through her problems. As a new Christian I really didn't know how to counsel her: I just kept telling her that Jesus Christ could meet her every need. Finally she settled down and agreed to wait one more day before taking the pills. As soon as Dottie hung up, I called her friend and told her of the conversation so she could check on Dottie later that evening.

That was my first actual experience counseling a person in crisis. I thought nothing about it in terms of my role in it, but Peggy, one of the women at the prayer meeting, said afterward, "Nell, you have a gift that God has given you to counsel people in crisis. I believe He will want you to use that gift." She identified a spiritual potential, and that encouraged me, though I didn't take it too seriously. After all, I was preparing to go to Africa.

Meanwhile, my new job provided a challenge. The medical constant care unit bustled with activity, and it seemed strange to have big people in the beds instead of little ones. They were old and young; they were on heart monitors and kidney machines. Some were dying, and both patients and families were often hysterical. But I worked hard to become the nurse I believed God wanted me to be. Though many areas of my life were still undisciplined, *above all*, for Jesus' sake, I wanted to be a really fine nurse.

One day shortly after I started working there, the head nurse on the unit told me she was going to be gone over the weekend.

"Will you assume my responsibilities while I'm gone?" she asked.

This request seemed a little unusual, because there were others who had seniority over me. Feeling inadequate to take such responsibility, yet knowing it was an honor to be asked, I accepted. I filled in for her on several occasions.

Then one day I was approached by one of the associate directors of nursing.

"Miss Collins," she said, "we'd like you to consider being head nurse of the unit on a permanent basis."

I was stunned.

"Oh, no. I couldn't."

"Please Miss Collins. You will make an excellent head nurse."

I stammered, "But . . . but . . . what I mean is . . . what I haven't been able to tell you . . . I'm a terrible nurse . . . you didn't know me before . . . what I am now is not what I was."

"Now, my dear," she said gently, "of course we know what kind of nurse you are. You came to us with the highest recommendation."

Gratitude overwhelmed me. *God* had given me this opportunity, and I knew it. Making my way down the hall to a vacant room, I knelt on the floor there and cried, thanking God for this miracle. He had given me a new heart, a clean start, and the opportunity to be a good nurse for His glory.

Through all this time, Mark and I continued dating,

though our relationship became more and more strained. He couldn't understand the change that had come into my life, and was exasperated that my interests were becoming so different from his.

I kept hoping that he would come to know the Lord and that he would want to go to Algeria, too. But he just kept saying, "It's okay for you, but keep me out of it."

For weeks I was torn, trying to rationalize to myself that once we got married I could get him to change his mind. But the Bible verse said, "Be ye not unequally yoked together with unbelievers. . . ." (2 Cor. 6:14).

I could not marry him.

I told Mark that I loved him but I couldn't see him any more. I expected to feel broken-hearted, but actually what I felt was a sense of anticipation. I was being obedient to God in breaking off our relationship, so I fully expected God to provide me with a good Christian husband. I daydreamed about serving in Africa with this wonderful man. What great things we would do for the Lord! Surely God would find me this perfect man very soon. At 25, I was not getting any younger, so there was no doubt He would come through for me in a short period of time.

VII

For four years I continued in the routine of working in the hospital and taking Bible school classes.

Immediately following my salvation, I saw God working in my life in many ways. Though I still had ups and downs, I no longer experienced deep depression or the desire to kill myself. I began interacting with people; each day held a *new promise*.

Still, something disturbed me. Besides forgiving my sin, I knew that God had given me two wonderful promises. One was that I would have *peace* and *rest* in my soul (Matt. 11:28), and the other was that He would make me a new creation (2 Cor. 5:17). For a while I did experience that wonderful peace of heart, and in the beginning I saw God changing me. He was working in many ways to give me victory over some of my bad habits and to help me develop some good ones.

Gradually, however, I became discouraged because I was not changing faster. In so many ways I was still the "old me." I still had my old thought patterns, my selfish motivations. I still had the inclination to sin and be in charge of my own life. I was still disorganized, undisciplined, and overweight.

In spite of all that, I continued to work toward becoming a missionary in Africa. At one point I needed a place to live, so Peggy, my friend from the prayer group, invited me to share her home for a few months until the final arrangements for Africa fell into place. Her husband and children graciously included me in their family for several months.

One night Peggy and I were going back to her house after prayer meeting.

"Peggy," I said, "I have the application papers to the Algerian mission right here in my purse. All I need to do is fill them out and send them in. But something is wrong, really wrong."

"What do you think it is?"

"I don't know. I really don't. Mother and Daddy are both sick, and my brother will be coming home soon from southeast Asia. My family needs me. On top of that, I need to get a lot of dental work done, and I don't have the money for it. . . ."

"I'll pray for you, Nell, that God will give you wisdom."

"I don't understand it, Peggy, but I think God is telling me not to go to Africa. I don't know why, but I just think I'm not supposed to go."

A few weeks later, I moved out of Peggy's house into my own apartment. For the first time in my life I had my own place with no family or roommates living with me.

I'm just going to forget the whole idea of becoming a missionary. If God couldn't even find a husband for me He must not be too interested in what I do. I'll just concentrate on getting more education in medicine. Perhaps I'll become a nurse-clinician; maybe I'll even go to medical school and become a doctor. . . .

I called the university and found that I could register the next week for classes.

But before the day of registration came, two little moles started itching on my back. Dr. Fitzpatrick removed them and a week later told me I had malignant melanoma.

My life came to a screeching halt. Peggy tried her best to console me, but a tidal wave of fear had overwhelmed me.

Peggy helped me pack my bag to go to the hospital for my surgery. She stuck my little red Bible in my suitcase—I hadn't opened it in weeks. She said, "We've got to trust the Lord, Nell. He knows what He's doing." She tried, really tried, to be comforting and helpful. But she didn't know that my heart was filled with resentment. She didn't know that I had been upset with God because He hadn't found a husband for me, or that now I was shaking my fist at God, saying, "What are You *doing* to me? How could You let this happen?"

Actually, these negative emotions had lingered just beneath the surface long before my cancer was diagnosed. When the cancer came, the thin veneer over those emotions was stripped off, and all my ugly feelings and horrible fears spilled out.

By the time I checked into the hospital Sunday evening, my anger and hysteria had changed to deep depression. I dragged my feet and did not speak to anyone except to answer questions for registration. I crawled into the hospital bed and turned my face to the wall. I knew that I was dying and that I would soon be standing face-to-face with God. I would have to give an account of what I had done with my life. My answer: "Not much."

I began praying in earnest.

"Dear God, what is happening to me? I'm so scared, and I don't know what is going on.

"My spiritual life has had the 'blahs' for a long time. I haven't had any joy or peace in so long I've forgotten what it's like.

"I know I belong to You, that I'm Your child, but that's all I know.

"All the time I've been in Bible school, I thought You would find a husband for me. I gave up Mark for You. . . ."

As I prayed, God showed me that I had been harboring resentment in my heart about Mark for a long time and

[71]

that resentment is sin. That is why I had been so miserable and unhappy in my Christian life, and it was the basic reason I wasn't maturing as a Christian.

I was able to talk with God about my fear of malignant melanoma, and I reached for my red Bible and started searching for comfort in His Word.

In Matthew 14: 25-33, I found a story I had heard many times before which suddenly took on a new meaning for me.

The disciples were out in a boat in a storm. The wind was fierce. Suddenly they saw Jesus coming to them, walking on the water. They were terrified.

Jesus said something like, "Cheer up. It's me. Don't be afraid."

Then Peter said, "If it's really You, then let me walk on the water to You."

And Peter walked on the water toward Jesus.

As long as he kept his eyes on Jesus, he was not afraid, and the Lord could give him power.

But then he took his eyes off Christ, and focused, instead, on his circumstances. When he concentrated on the wind and the waves and the storm, he became afraid and started sinking.

That is what I had done.

When I first trusted Christ four years before, I experienced real peace in my heart. Little by little, however, I allowed my focus to get *off* Jesus and *on* my circumstances.

Like Peter, I had experienced a glorious time of looking only to Jesus. I, too, had "walked on the water" in a sense. But, again like Peter, I took my eyes off Jesus and started looking at my earthly problems rather than the *spiritual* solutions.

Peter saw the storm; I saw my problems of sick parents, dental bills, no husband, and, now, melanoma.

Peter became afraid and started sinking. Concentrating on my problems, I, too, began to sink into doubt, fear, anger, and hysteria.

As I read this story once again, I began to realize that God had taught me an important concept. I knew that as long as I focused on Jesus, I would not be afraid.

For the first time in four years, I again experienced God's peace. I still believed that I was going to die within a few weeks, but I knew that death could only usher me into the very presence of Jesus, and that was exciting.

I may not have a week, I thought, *I might not even live through the day. But today, just today, I want to be just as close to Jesus as I can be. For as long as God gives me, as long as I have breath in my lungs and a functioning brain, all I want to do is tell people about Jesus Christ and the peace that is possible through Him. I want to tell people that He can bring brightness to any dark valley.*

As I went through the next days, I found that I needed the strength and confidence that comes from God to endure the "storm" while focusing on Jesus all the while.

The next morning before they wheeled me into surgery, a doctor came to see me.

"Our greatest concern, Nell," he said, "is with the depth of the invasion of melanoma cells. We don't know how far they have penetrated, so we are going to scoop out a large area all around the site of the mole so that, hopefully, we can remove every melanoma cell." Then he told me that they were going to remove flesh from my back the size and depth of a saucer. Then they would graft skin from the upper front of my thigh. When I woke, I'd hurt both places.

Following the surgery, for a couple of days I drifted in and out of sleep, groggy from the pain medication. Mom came to see me. She tried not to show how frightened she was, and I felt bad for causing her so much grief.

"Mom," I said, "why don't you go on home and take care of yourself and Daddy? It's going to be a long haul here, and I'm in good hands. Please go."

The first time out of bed I felt like an old woman, stooped over, light-headed, and queasy. Aides held me up on each side as I stumbled into the bathroom, wearing a skimpy hospital gown. The flourescent lights made everything seem unreal, as if all this were happening to somebody else.

As a patient I learned much about nursing. Though many of the nurses were kind and gentle to me, some seemed cold and uncaring. I cringed when I heard a nurse in the hall talk about "the melanoma in 44 by the window."

I wanted to shout at her and say, "I'm not a melanoma: I'm Nell, I'm a person, and I want somebody to care!" Then I wondered how many times I had called a person "the renal failure" or "the coronary."

I saw how nurses and others tried to meet spiritual needs with physical remedies. What I needed was encouragement to focus on Jesus, but literally everyone and everything in the hospital experience focused on my physical problems.

Some visitors actually did more harm than good. One visitor came in, chattering incessantly, as though she could not bear the silence. "Now don't you look just wonderful," she lied. That was upsetting, because I knew I looked horrible. "You don't look at all like my aunt who had melanoma. Why, my dear, she just got these horrible black knots all over her body. Of course she died." Then she prattled on about something else, never even knowing how much she had upset me with those words so very descriptive of melanoma. She actually thought that she was helping.

A pastor came in and asked me about my surgery, and quoted a Bible verse to me. He was aloof, detatched, and did not even get close to finding out my emotional needs. He was not really concerned about me. I had the feeling he just wanted to check me off his list.

My hospital friends and the women from the prayer group were wonderful to call and stop in to see me. They filled my room with cards and other expressions of love, and I appreciated everything they did.

What seemed hardest for anyone to do was to simply come quietly into my world and take my hand and let me cry. People appeared so concerned with "What am I going to say?" that they could not or would not let me express my fears. I didn't want preaching or platitudes. I wanted an "alongsider," someone who would walk with me through difficult days.

The second day after surgery, they helped me out of bed so I could sit up in a chair for a few minutes twice a day. One time, after sitting back against the chair, I leaned forward to get something from my tray. Panic! I buzzed the nurse.

"Nurse!" I called. Then I turned my head to the side and sniffed, trying to find the source of a terrible odor.

In a few minutes the nurse sauntered into the room. "What is it?"

"It's my back," I said. "I leaned forward just now and it felt like my whole back, dressing and all, had stuck to the chair. And the smell! It smells terrible, like something crawled up in there and died!"

"Now, now," she said soothingly. "It's nothing to worry about. It's just a part of the healing process. You'll be getting the dressing off soon and everything will be just fine."

I mentioned my concerns again a time or two, but everyone reassured me that it was nothing.

Then the day finally came for the surgeon to remove the dressing and check the graft. He had told me previously that he hoped for a 75 to 80 percent "take."

I stretched out on the bed, again with my backside up and my face to the wall. The place on my thigh where the skin had been removed for the graft hurt unbearably as I lay on it. The doctor stood by my bed with a trash can at his side. The wound on my back resembled a small pizza and each piece of skin to be grafted had been placed on like pieces of pepperoni. The doctor reached over to my back and plucked at something, then turned and, *plunk*, dropped it in the trash can. Again he reached over and *plunk*. Into the trash can. Plunk. Plunk. Plunk.

Finally I realized that those little pepperoni-like pieces of skin were plunking into the trash can.

"Nell," he said slowly, "I hate to have to tell you this . . ."

Here I am again, I thought, *on my belly getting more bad news.*

". . . but not one piece of the graft 'took.' You have a pseudomonas infection which we'll have to eliminate before we go back into surgery for another graft."

An infection! That must have been the smell.

My nursing background came in handy during the treatment for the infection. The doctor left orders for the dressing to be wet down with antiseptic solution every two hours.

Two hours later, a couple of nurses came in and ripped off the bandages so they could wet down the gauze.

"Hey, wait a minute, girls," I said. "There's got to be a better way. I can't stand having that tape pulled off every two hours." Now I felt more confident. Every day in my job I helped figure out problems like this one.

"All we need to do," I said, "is leave the dressing on and lay a rubber catheter on top of it. Get one of those catheters with a tiny beveled hole on the side so the solution can flow gently out of the tube. Then cover it up with more layers of gauze and tape the whole thing down, leaving the tip of the catheter sticking out. Then all you'll have to do every two hours is take an asepto syringe and squirt in the antiseptic solution."

They thought that was a great idea, and brought in other aides and nurses to show them how we had solved the problem. They could use that technique whenever necessary.

I thought, as I waited there in the hospital, how very much this infection was like sin in the life. The infection prevented the graft from "taking"; sin prevents the Christian from growing. The infection must be "cleaned up" before the surgeon can work; sin must be confessed and placed under the blood of Jesus before God can work in the life of a believer.

After the second graft I was not allowed to get up for two days. I could not move around. They mummified me with one arm tied down at my side so that I could not move the shoulder blade and disturb the graft. I had to lie face down, and the big wounds on the front of both legs hurt worse than my back.

My biggest problem was going to the bathroom. I couldn't get up, and lying face down, a bedpan did not do the job. The nurses came in and shook their heads, "How are we going to get this girl to void?" They preferred not to use a catheter, unless there was no other choice. Finally I thought of it. I had been doing pushups at home for a few weeks before going into the hospital. I could do a one-armed pushup and we could use a kidney-shaped emesis basin as a bedpan. It worked! Such a relief.

For days, when in bed, I could only lie face down. I kept my red Bible in front of me all morning and studied the word with a hunger I had not known before.

Though I knew rough days stretched before me, every day I gained more confidence in the God who makes no mistakes. I found a verse in Psalms that helped me under-

stand how God could use my three weeks in the hospital:
"It is good for me that I have been afflicted, that I might
learn thy statutes (Ps. 119:71)." In the valley of affliction is
the brightness of His word.

VIII

Much to my surprise, within a few months I had recuperated enough from surgery to go back to work. Although I didn't die during my hospital stay, as I thought I would, dying from the melanoma remained a real and ever-present possibility.

At the elevator that morning, the nurses on my floor crowded around me, hugging me and smiling, making me feel loved and appreciated. It was good to be back.

"Today I buy your lunch," said my friend Katy with a grin.

As we entered the cafeteria at noon, I sensed that Katy wanted to have a talk, a serious talk, but I waited for her to speak. We made our way to a table in the corner, away from the groups of other nurses.

"I . . well . . I've been hearing good things, Nell," she started falteringly.

"Really?"

"Well, you know. About your surgery. I hear they got it all."

I shrugged. "Well, you know how it is with cancer. You never know for sure."

"But . . . well . . . the outlook is good, isn't it?"

"To tell the truth, Katy, I don't really know. I could be just fine and never have another problem with it. On the other hand, if there are melanoma cells running around in my body, if they missed even one of them, then it will be like a time-bomb ticking inside of me. I might be fine for a while, but someday the bomb will explode. I've seen melanoma before, Katy. It's a mean one. I really don't believe that I have very long to live."

"Oh, Nell . . ." Katy said, tears welling up in her eyes.

"Now cut that out, silly," I laughed. "There's no need to cry. I'm not worried, and I'm not scared. I have personally received Jesus Christ as my Savior, so I know that God loves me, and that He is in control. Nothing can happen in my life unless He determines that it is for *my* good and His glory.

By this time Katy was smiling, too.

"The really fantastic thing, Katy," I continued, "is that it's okay *no matter what happens!* It's really *okay,* do you know what I mean? I'm not afraid anymore. *I'm not afraid to live, and I'm not afraid to die.* I know that Jesus lives within me, and He'll never leave me. If I have to suffer some more, that's okay, because I know Jesus has a purpose in it, and He will be with me every step of the way. If I die, that's okay too. He'll just be taking me home a little sooner, that's all. God has given me tremendous peace, and I praise Him for it."

Katy had told me earlier that she was not a Christian, so she did not really understand what I was talking about. "I don't know your God," she said, "but I'd sure like to have that kind of peace." Katy and I worked together frequently, and often talked about the Lord.

Alice, another friend at the hospital, worked upstairs, and we met for coffee nearly every day. A sweet Christian who had several grown children, she was a friend I leaned on for emotional support. One day we happened to meet in the large, walk-in linen closet.

"Alice," I said, "I keep having the strangest feelings. On one hand, God is granting me real peace, a confidence in *Him,* knowing that He is perfect and whatever He allows in my life is also perfect, and that gives me real peace."

"Then what's wrong?" she asked, loading a stack of sheets onto a utility cart.

"It's this sense of *urgency* I feel. So many people are on the brink of eternity and I want to tell everybody I see about Jesus Christ. I want to talk with everybody—everybody *except* cancer patients, that is."

"You don't want to talk with cancer patients?"

"I can't, Alice, it's just too hard. They've got what I've got, you see. I'm sure the Lord understands."

"The Lord *always* understands, Nell. He knows exactly how you feel. But I think you'd better talk to Him about it."

I did just that for several months, studying God's Word and asking His direction in my life.

Then one day Dr. Greene came up to me at the nurse's station.

"Nell," he said, "I've got a patient named Eddie in 1504A. He's got the same kind of cancer you have, except he's not going to make it. Would you be my ambassador and go see him? He is so depressed, and I think you could help him."

Flattered to be Dr. Greene's ambassador, I agreed.

I walked into Eddie's room and said, "Hi, Eddie! I'm Nell. I'm a friend of Dr. Greene, and I promised him I'd come in and see how you were doing."

He looked up at me with sad, sad eyes, and it suddenly hit me that here I was talking with a cancer patient! *I don't want to talk with a cancer patient. Lord!* I panicked. *What am I doing here? I can't talk with a cancer patient.*

Then I thought, *or can I?*

God had allowed me to be trained as a nurse and in Bible college. He had even allowed me to face cancer in my own life. Could it be that He was going to use me to minister in a very special way?

A Scripture verse flashed through my mind:

"Now, then, we are ambassadors for Christ, as though

[*81*]

God did beseech you by us: we pray you in Christ's stead, be ye reconciled to God" (2 Cor. 5:20).

I've known all along, I thought, *that we are to be ambassadors for Christ. I've been giving Him all kinds of excuses about why I can't be His ambassador to cancer patients. But when Dr. Greene asks me to do that, I'm flattered to go.*

I prayed, "Lord, I'm willing, but don't know *how.* Please show me *how* to help this man."

Then, for the first time, I took a good look at Eddie. He wasn't a "cancer patient." He was a *person.* A real person with a family, a job, bills to pay, and a life to live. He was a man with hopes and dreams and ambitions, just like anybody else.

A big guy, Eddie looked as though he had been a football player. He was bandaged all over from his surgery that morning. He was low, really low. And hurting.

I asked him about his incision, which circled up under his arm and down his side. He grimaced in pain.

"This is a hard day, isn't it?" I said softly. I had learned when I was in a hospital bed that the need is for quiet understanding, not preaching, not platitudes, and not lies about looking "wonderful."

With my simple question, the flood gates broke down. I had never seen a football player cry, but Eddie put his face in his hands and sobbed.

I didn't even understand what I was doing, but in that visit I met him at the point of his need: his physical problems and his emotional response. He was not ready for me to get into any heavy discussion of spiritual matters. As I left, all I said was, "I'll be praying for you, Eddie."

"Thanks," he said, "I'll be needing it."

I left Eddie's room knowing I would be back. It was scary, talking with someone who had cancer, *my* kind of cancer, even. But God gave me the courage to see Eddie every day. Soon I met Margie, Eddie's wife. With two young children and a dying husband, she was terrified. All the time Eddie was in the hospital, we talked in generalities. We talked more about his physical problems than anything else. Slowly but steadily, bridges were built. Eddie and Margie gained confidence in me. They began to trust me. When he was released, Margie gave me their home telephone number. I saw Eddie at home the first time on a Saturday, my day off. Eddie's brother, a college student and a professed atheist who thought he had all the answers, also was visiting.

Seeing a hospital patient in his home was unexpectedly strange for me. I was accustomed to white sheets and no distractions. The confusion of relatives visiting, the telephone ringing, and kids squabbling jangled my sense of hospital orderliness. But after many visits, I got used to it.

Staying close to the entire family, I visited often. Eddie, Margie, and I had long talks at Eddie's bedside. Margie and I baked biscuits and cried together while making Eddie's favorite cookies. I helped the kids make candles in the garage. I quizzed them on their homework, tucked them into bed at night, and answered their questions of, "What will happen if Daddy dies?"

I attempted to point them to spiritual values on a number of occasions. They were interested and fairly open, but not yet ready to make any personal decisions regarding their relationships with Christ.

Eddie asked questions. "How can a loving God allow me to hurt like this? Why would He let me get too sick to work and provide for my family? Doesn't He care?"

We talked and talked, consistently moving in the right direction. But Eddie had not yet accepted Christ.

Then late one night the telephone rang. Margie's voice sounded high-pitched and strained. "Nell," she said, "Eddie's back in the hospital. It's gone to his brain."

I was trembling. *Oh, God, please help him to understand your plan of salvation before it's too late. Please, God, please.* I knew, too, that the time would come that he simply would be too ill to make a real decision for the Lord. Even as I prayed, I feared the worst. I could not bring him any hope when I saw him the next day, if he still wanted to "go it alone" without the Lord.

The telephone at the nurse's station was ringing when I arrived a few minutes early for work the next day.

"Nell," a familiar voice said, "It's Eddie. I need to see you."

"Be right there," I whispered into the telephone. I tore up the stairs and burst into Eddie's room. There he was, sitting up in bed with his Bible open and tears streaming down his face.

"I want God to save me, Nell." Through the tears we rejoiced.

He knew that he was a sinner, that Christ had died for his sin. He wanted to receive Jesus into his heart as Savior and Lord.

I asked, "Would you like for me to help you pray? All you need to do is talk to God about it."

After Eddie prayed, inviting Jesus Christ to come into his heart, he smiled and said: "Thanks, Nell. It's okay now. Whatever happens, I'm not afraid anymore."

When Eddie died a few weeks later, the funeral was one of victory and joy. The pastor of a Bible-believing church gave the funeral message and the people from that church offered love and friendship to Margie and the children. Many people came to know the Lord as a result of Eddie's salvation.

The day after Eddie's funeral, I got a call from Margie's friend, whose next-door neighbor had cancer and was extremely depressed. Would I go see her? Then someone else called about a favorite aunt who had leukemia. My telephone rang again. And again. God had given me a ministry.

By the end of that year I was seeing 25 cancer patients

regularly, and by the next year it was 50. By the end of the third year, I was trying to see 100 people. Every evening and weekend I was with "my people." The lack of time frustrated me, because I only could see cancer patients in my time off from work. Emotionally and financially the strain increased daily, and I was exhausted from squeezing too many hours into each day.

My visits home became less and less frequent. One day Mom said in a note to me, "Guess I'll have to get cancer before you'll come and see me."

So I went home. Dad sat in the corner, as usual, in his big chair. He looked lonely.

"I understand you are visiting cancer patients in your free time. That sounds very depressing."

It was the most he had said to me in a long time.

"Well, Daddy," I said, "it would be depressing, but I am bringing those people real hope."

He looked at me blankly.

"Daddy, what I am telling people is that they can have a relationship with Jesus Christ. It's not just a ritual or religion."

"Nelia Anne," he said, "I have spent most of my life serving the Lord, and I am still confused about what it all means." Poor Daddy. No wonder he had always seemed so unhappy.

That night I lay in bed and prayed for him. I knew he had been miserable and unhappy his whole life, and I felt at a loss to help him. But I determined to let him know that I appreciated the ways he had been a positive influence on my life. For example, he had encouraged me to sing, and he had taught me to play the piano by chording. Music became an important part of my life, and I wanted to thank Daddy for teaching me how to enjoy it.

Back on the job, I continued to squeeze visits to cancer patients into every available hour. The urgency was real. Several of "my people" already had died, and I felt that I must see as many people as possible in the time I had left.

One night I was going to have dinner with Peggy and her family, and Peggy met me at the door. I knew by the look on her face that something was wrong.

"Nell," she said, "I got a call from your Mom just now. When she got no answer at your place, she called here."

"What's wrong? What happened?"

"It's your dad, Nell. He died this morning. Your mom said he was out taking a walk and he just fell dead with a heart attack." *Daddy's gone. And I never told him 'Thank You.' My heart ached.*

I went right home to be with Mom. She was more distraught than I had ever seen her. I tried to comfort her, but felt as though I had failed Daddy. He had spiritual needs and he died struggling with them. His death only increased the sense of urgency I felt to help people before it was too late.

As each day passed, I found it harder and harder to devote so many hours to my job when cancer patients had such a desperate need. A man in Terre Haute with lung cancer was so depressed that he refused to talk with anyone in his family, but he had agreed to talk to me. A woman in Ft. Wayne was hysterical because she had just discovered that her cancer had metastasized to her bones. I needed to go to them; I *wanted* to be with them. I had so little time.

At the hospital I was frustrated, too, because as a staff worker I felt that I could only talk in generalities to people who were patients there. I could only visit patients after work hours, and I needed to go out of town to see people in the evenings and on the weekends. It broke my heart when I couldn't visit a patient in need. Where would I find the time?

I started praying specifically about my needs. Trying to continue as I was didn't make sense emotionally or financially. The pace exhausted me, and my schedule left no time for anything but work.

"Lord," I prayed, "I need wisdom and counsel. Please bring someone to me who can help me figure out my life."

Exactly two weeks to the day, Sally Williams called.

She and the other missionaries had been sent home from the country in Africa where she had served, and now she was working with students on a university campus in another state.

"Nell," she said, "I need to talk with you. My mother is in the hospital in Indianapolis, and I'm coming to see her. Will you meet me in mom's room, then go have coffee with me?"

I adjusted my schedule so I could meet Sally. We had often shared concerns about our mothers because they were both ill with diabetic heart failure. Over the years we had visited in each others' homes, so Sally's Mom was my friend, too. We had a good visit with her before heading down to the cafeteria.

After we settled into the booth with our coffee, Sally looked at me with the same expression she had had on her face when she confronted me about singing in the trio twelve years before.

"Nell," she said, "I need to talk with you about a serious matter, but I'm afraid it will destroy our lifetime friendship."

"Nothing can destroy our friendship, Sally. Shoot."

She sipped her coffee and cleared her throat.

"I know that you dearly love nursing, Nell, that outside of the Lord it is your whole life. You are a good nurse, and God is using you as a nurse. But for two solid weeks the Lord has been dealing with *me* about *your* work."

"*My* work?" I asked. I had no idea what she was trying to say.

"Yes," she said, "your work with cancer patients. I really believe that God is directing you into a tremendously important ministry with people who are suffering greatly, both physically and emotionally. Have you ever considered working with cancer patients in a full-time way?"

"No," I said, "not really. Except a few weeks ago something did happen that I didn't really understand. A woman came to see me from a group that works with cancer patients, asking me to take the job of coordinating all the patients in her area. At first I thought it sounded great, because I'd have access to the names and addresses of hundreds of cancer patients."

"What did you tell her?"

"Well," I said, "I explained to her that my purpose in visiting cancer patients was to bring them spiritual hope and resources, and that my hope is in a personal relationship with Jesus Christ. She said that theirs was a secular group and that I could not present the gospel message to patients, but she still wanted me to take the job. I told her I'd think about it. It was tempting, in a sense, to have access to all these people, but I knew that I couldn't go to see a dying person and not tell him about Jesus."

Sally looked at me intently. "It sounds as though you made a wise decision."

"I don't really understand it, but I know that 1 Corinthians 3:11 says that the only worthy foundation is Jesus Christ. I couldn't see cancer patients on any other basis."

"But still," Sally said, "I believe that God has something really special in mind for you. You spent four years thinking that God wanted you to go to Africa, but apparently He had other plans. I don't think He ever wanted you in Africa; I think that He was preparing you all along for a ministry with cancer patients. You were so upset with God for not bringing you a Christian husband after you broke up with Mark, but because you are single you'll have much more time and energy to pour into the work."

"Right now," I said, "I don't have enough of either time or energy. But how can I see cancer patients full-time? I've got rent to pay and food to buy. And it costs a lot of money to drive all over the state to see people."

"I don't see why you couldn't work with a mission board and raise support like any other missionary. But you'd have to give up your job."

My job! I had often wished I could spend 24 hours a day with cancer patients, but I'd never really considered giving up my job to do it.

My job meant a great deal to me. I *loved* nursing and I knew I was a good nurse. The pay and prestige of being head nurse would be hard to relinquish.

"Would you be willing to consider it?" Sally asked.

My answer was a willing "yes." I knew that God had answered my prayer. This was His way of giving to me the desire of my heart—the *time* I needed to see cancer patients.

Sally took the information about me to her mission board, and they were interested in backing this new ministry, though it would take several months, maybe even a year, to work out the details.

Such a long time to wait! I thought. *I might not even be here several months from now.*

I felt a need to discuss the whole matter with my pastor, Wendell T. Heller. "You know, Nell," he said, "God never leads us to any place where His lessons cannot be learned. He has given you a tremendous resource in your own suffering. In 2 Corinthians He tells us that He comforts us so that we can, in turn, comfort others."

Then he surprised me.

"I'd like for you to consider having the board of this local church be your mission board in this ministry. We can work out the details quickly. You need to give the hospital thirty days notice. I see no reason why you couldn't start this work on a full-time basis within the next few weeks."

I agreed to consider it and to pray about it, but I was at a loss to know what to do. Should I go with the established mission board or work with my local church? I had often told people that God guides us through His Word, but I knew, too, that the Bible did not contain the names of specific mission boards and churches. How would I ever know which board to choose?

The very next morning in my devotions a verse jumped off the page at me:

"Say not ye, There are yet *four months,* and then cometh harvest? behold, I say unto you, Lift up your eyes, and look on the fields: *for they are white already to harvest"* (John 4:35—emphasis mine).

God had directed me through His Word! Why should I wait four months or longer? *The fields are white already to harvest!* God was telling me to go ahead with my local church as my mission board.

The board worked out a budget for me which was to be supplied each month by churches and individuals. I did not have quite enough financial backing to fully support the ministry at the end of thirty days, so I continued to work one night a week at the hospital. In time God began dealing with my heart. The hospital job represented "security" to me, and I looked to that job to bail me out if things got rough. But knowing that I needed to totally trust the Lord to provide all my support, I left my hospital job for good.

In all the years since I have been a full-time missionary without an outside source of income, God has met my needs every day. In months when my regular support did not come in, random love gifts have made up the difference.

The Lord often has surprised me with totally unexpected blessings. The dental work that had, in part, kept me from going to Africa still was not done because it would cost $2000, and I did not have that kind of money.

One evening I was giving a report to one of my supporting churches, and one of the men in the congregation came up to me after the service.

"This may seem like an odd question, Nell," he said, "but I'm wondering if you need some bridgework done."

I must have looked totally shocked, because he laughed and continued, "I'm a dental technician, so I notice things like that." He must have been referring to my missing teeth! "I make bridgework and crowns for dentists, so if you'll have your dentist call me, I'd like to provide what you need without charge to you." He handed me his card and all I could utter was an incredulous "Thank you!"

A dentist in my local church then offered to provide all of my other dental work without charge, and I marveled at the way the Lord works. When I thanked my dentist he just said, "This is just one small way I can serve the Lord."

Another time I needed a car desperately, and a car dealer made a fine automobile available to me at his cost.

Every year a cancer patient buys my AAA Motor Club membership for me and she says, "It's just a little something I can do."

Women in my supporting churches regularly have sewn for me and given me haircuts without charge, and others supply me with cologne and other personal "niceties" that I would not go out and buy for myself.

Unknown to me, one of my cancer patients had a diamond ring in her lockbox. Before her mother died, she had requested that her daughter keep the ring until a special person came along who would really appreciate it. Much to my surprise, she decided that I was that special person. It seems that ministering to me has become a ministry for these people.

Whenever I'm tempted to worry about whether God will supply my needs, I just look back and marvel at what He has already done.

IX

Instead of dying with cancer, I began *living* with cancer every day, every moment of my life. I lived with my own diagnosis of cancer, to be sure, but beyond that, my life became intertwined with hundreds, even thousands of people who had cancer of every type and description.

Eddie had been my first patient, and I had prayed that God would show me how to meet his needs, and He did. I became aware that every person with cancer faces a unique medical situation. The type of cancer, its location, its extent, and its rate of growth are crucial factors. The person's family situation, financial condition, and mental attitude, I discovered, have impact on the situation. But every person with cancer, I concluded, is one with great needs which can only be met by Jesus Christ.

I remember Eleanor Smith. At the time I met her, she had been waging war with cancer for several years. The cancer had started in her breasts, then showed up in her lungs. She had just been told that it had gone to her bones. As a new Christian, she had many questions, and I visited her frequently in her home.

One day when I knocked on the door, she called out, "Come on in, Nell." When she saw me she said, "I'm afraid." The tears flowed down her cheeks and she sobbed.

I held her hand. "That's okay, Eleanor. Go ahead and

cry. God gave us tears and it sometimes helps to let them out." I thought as Eleanor cried how important it is to have contact with a person in the early stages of their cancer before it has had time to spread. If I'd have known Eleanor during the several years since her cancer was first diagnosed, we'd have been able to work through so many of her questions and to prepare her to face the hard days ahead.

She wiped her eyes. "Why don't you fix us a cup of tea?" she finally said. I went into the kitchen and turned on the stove under the teakettle.

"I've tried everything, Nell, and God isn't answering my prayers. I've prayed that He would heal me and I just get sicker. What am I doing wrong, Nell? I guess I just don't have enough faith."

"Eleanor," I said, "it's not how much faith you have, it's in whom you have placed your faith. He doesn't want us to have faith in healing. He wants us to have faith in Him. If we trust Him to be absolutely perfect in His dealings with us, knowing that He might have an eternal purpose even higher than physical healing, then that allows us to face the future with confidence."

I showed her the passage in Hebrews 11 that tells of believers who saw great miracles in their earthly lives: kingdoms conquered, the mouths of lions shut, fires miraculously quenched, and even the dead resurrected (vs. 33-35).

"But if you read on, Eleanor," I said, "you'll see that other believers suffered greatly and did not see a miracle in a physical sense. They were tortured, beaten, imprisoned, stoned, sawn in two, and they lost every physical comfort they had known, including their homes (vs. 35-38). These people had just as much faith as those who saw miracles, but God used their trials in a different way."

"You mean," Eleanor said, "that God may have a purpose in my *not* getting well?"

"That's exactly what I mean. God is perfect in all of His dealings with us, and our job is to simply be willing to be used to God's glory."

"God can't use me. I'm too sick. I can't even fix supper for my family or wash a dish. I can't do anything for God."

By this time the teakettle was whistling, so I went to the kitchen and fixed us each a cup of tea.

While we sipped our tea, I showed Eleanor a little something I had written to help me face the adversities of life:

MY PURPOSE

My purpose in living—
    To know Christ and to make Him known.
My purpose in suffering—
    To show Christ strong.
My purpose in dying—
    To be ushered into His very presence,
    and stay there forever.

"You see Eleanor, my choice for my life would be that I be well and active and able to be in 'high gear,' driving from one end of the state to the other, telling everyone I can about the Lord Jesus. But if suffering comes, then I have to adapt and shift down into 'low gear.' If I'm flat out on a hospital bed, unable to even get up to go to the bathroom, then I can't operate in 'high gear.'

"When I'm in 'low gear,'" I said, "it only frustrates me to think about all the things I could do if I were well. The only solution is to *consciously* change gears. Get into 'low gear' and think: How can I glorify God in this situation? How can I show Christ strong? Sometime I might be too sick to do anything, even pray. If I'm too sick to talk, I can put my Bible on my bedside table. Just having my Bible there will speak to people.

"If I have to go to the hospital," I continued, "it's never an accident or random chance that I'm assigned to a certain floor with a particular roommate and have contact with individual doctors and nurses. God brings them to me and me to them to give me an opportunity to 'make Him known' or 'show Him strong' until He 'ushers me into His presence.'"

Eleanor smiled and I hugged her. I wrote out a copy of "My Purpose" and put it beside her on the coffee table.

"I'll be back in a few days, Eleanor," I said as I left, and we were able to have many good visits in the weeks that followed.

Another time I was asked to see George Eakins, a man in his seventies, who was dying with prostate cancer. We talked casually, and he was pleasant and polite to me. I mistakenly assumed, because he was a mild-mannered man, that he was a Christian. But when I asked if I could read a few Bible verses to him, this 'nice' man turned on me and exploded.

"Listen, lady," he snarled at me, "I'm going to heaven, and I don't need your Jesus."

On the way home I cried and cried. *I blew it,* I thought. *I moved in too fast to spiritual matters, and now I may never get another chance to talk with him about the Lord.*

I went back to my office and prayed, "Oh, Lord, if only he could see . . ."

Then I stopped. *SEE! That's it! I need to help him visualize what God has done for him! But how?*

Getting out a stack of index cards, scissors, and tape, I thought how simple is God's message to us. Drawing stick figures and taping the cards together, I came up with a simple, visual way to share the gospel. I didn't know if George would ever let me show it to him, but I prayed that God would give me the opportunity.

For the next several weeks, I stayed in touch with the family and sent George cards and talked with his wife on the telephone. We talked only about his physical condition and I didn't even mention spiritual matters. Then one day George's wife called. "Nell," she said, "can you come to see George? His emotions are out of control. We just can't handle his emotions. Please come."

I didn't know if he would let me show it to him, but I stuck into my purse the little index-card visual, just in case.

It had been three months since I last saw him, and he looked as if he had aged fifty years. I hardly recognized him. He was propped up by pillows on a hospital bed on the porch.

For a few minutes he didn't speak, he just cried.

His first words were, "Nell, God has made my heart soft. Tell me how I can know Him like you do."

I reached into my purse and pulled out my little illustration and just talked through it with him.

"This little picture shows that God—represented by the triangle—created each one of us. In the beginning, God's first people had a close, intimate fellowship with Him with nothing hindering. God gave people freedom of choice, however, and the first people chose to go their own way instead of God's way.

"The sin of disobedience and rebellion caused a great barrier, separating all of humanity from God.

"People try, really try, to reach God by doing all kinds of good things. The arrows represent the good things a person might try to do: going to church, getting baptized, and so on. But *man's efforts* can't break through the barrier of sin.

"That's why Jesus Christ had to come to earth and shed His blood for my sin and your sin. All we have to do is accept what God has already done for us and receive Christ by faith. He will wrap us in a robe of righteousness. From that moment on we can know that when God looks at us He doesn't see our sin, He sees the righteousness of Christ."

That day George Eakins received Jesus Christ as his personal Savior.

Four days later his wife called again. "Nell," she said, "George is upset. Can you come and see him again? He's got some questions."

I went straight to his house and Mrs. Eakins took me out to the porch where George was still in bed.

"I just have one question, Nell," he said. "I know that I'm satisfied with my Savior, but I don't know if He's satisfied with me."

I took another index card out of my purse. This time it was a plain one. I wrote out a verse in big letters:

"(GOD IS) JUST, AND THE JUSTIFIER OF HIM WHICH BELIEVETH IN JESUS" (Rom. 3:26).

George read it out loud, snapped his fingers and said, "That does it! That's all I needed to know." Then he lay back in his bed with an expression of absolute peace on his face.

During the next weeks he lived and breathed that single verse. He told his wife that when he died he wanted that index card buried with him. At his funeral Mrs. Eakins placed it near him for all to see. There was grief, but there was also victory.

Sometimes it has been possible for me to get to know cancer patients just after diagnosis, and often we are blessed with years of friendship and opportunity to learn more about our wonderful Savior.

Allison, a young married woman fighting Hodgkin's disease, was a Christian with an on-again, off-again spiritual experience. We started having a weekly, one-on-one Bible study, to learn some of the basics of the Christian life. We talked about the importance of daily Bible study and prayer, and she said, "But Nell, when I try to read the Bible I just get all mixed up. It's too hard to understand."

"Well," I said, "in my own life I've found that I need a systematic approach to studying the Bible. Otherwise I'm too likely to let it get crowded out of my schedule. I use the daily devotional, *Our Daily Bread* (available free of charge from Radio Bible Class, Grand Rapids, Michigan 49555). At the top of each page it suggests a portion of Scripture to read. So each day I read that passage and then write it out in my own words."

Opening the Bible to the familiar Psalm 23, we worked through the verses.

Psalm 23: 1-6

I. General Understanding of Verses

1. The Lord of Heaven is my personal Shepherd. Because of Him I will know nothing of dissatisfaction or un-fulfillment.

2. He feeds me in the comfort of thick, green pasture grass, and gives me rest in it beside the quiet brooks of water.

3. He revives and restores my spirit. He guides, directs, and leads me in the life-style and patterns of rightness for the sake of His name.

4. Even in the "valley of the shadow" of impending death—

   —NO FEAR, because
   a. God is with me
   b. God's Words comfort me. And that makes the valley *bright* and gives me . . .

5. Hope!
   —because
   a. God is preparing a banquet table for me
   b. The Holy Spirit lives within me
   c. My cup of blessing is full

6. In life: Goodness and mercy of God
   In death: I will spend eternity in His presence.

In later visits I taught Allison to investigate the verses, looking for areas of disobedience, principles of Scripture, and commands for us to obey. Finally I showed her how to personalize the verses so they would speak directly to her.

Each time I came to visit, we went over our devotions and talked about any questions she had. It was a time of growing, learning, and maturing in the Lord. When she went through difficult days of radiation and chemotherapy, she was able to face them with confidence, leaning on the Lord every step of the way.

X

Early in my cancer ministry, I felt as though my patients and I were in the same boat. They rowed on their side, and I rowed on mine, but we were in it together. God taught me, and I was able to pass on what I'd learned to others. God knew that I had to learn to deal with worry and discouragement myself if I were going to be able to help other people face their fears.

God allowed me to have a particularly insidious type of cancer. Melanoma is an unpredictable disease. It can be removed surgically and never cause another problem. However, even one microscopic melanoma cell remaining after surgery can travel through the body, multiplying rampantly, establishing new tumors. Melanoma cells can travel through the blood and lymphatic systems to any part of the body, including the bones and vital organs. Invasion of the vital organs interferes with normal functioning, and that is what ultimately causes death.

Melanoma cells, if left in the body, might not multiply and invade vital organs right away. These mysterious cells can lie dormant for months, years, or even decades before becoming active again. That is why a melanoma patient who seems to be doing well never knows for sure if one day it will go out of control again.

For me, it has been learning to live with the dark, ever-present fear that I might wake up one morning and find an ominous lump which will reveal that my melanoma is out of control. It is learning to live with the knowledge that one of my regular hospital checkups, with scans of the liver, brain, and bone, might reveal an internal melanoma growth.

After my surgery I had a checkup with Dr. Fitzpatrick, and he laid it out for me.

"It is going to be your responsibility," he said, "to keep a close watch of moles on your body. I want you to look for any malignant changes. You should watch for irregularity, a color change, the development of a center in the mole, or some other change in appearance. You need also to look for new moles or moles that just look strange. It is even more important that you watch for lumps, bumps or bulges under the skin."

"What do I do if I see any of this kind of thing?"

"If you see something that looks drastically wrong, call me immediately. If it's a mole that just looks suspicious, then watch it for a month. If you see a malignant change within that month, call me, and I'll take a look at it."

It may not sound like much, to have to be constantly watching moles and lumps and bumps, but it can drag a person into a deep depression unless it is combatted on a spiritual level.

Shortly after I had this conversation with Dr. Fitzpatrick, I was driving home from seeing a patient and I happened to look at my left arm. That mole! It looked different. A little darker, perhaps a little bigger. My heart started pounding, and I felt clammy. My chest tightened and I felt unable to breathe. I was still an hour from Indianapolis, and all the way home I was in a state of panic. I drove too fast, but I was hurrying home so I could pray about it and "turn it over" to the Lord.

When I finally got home I dashed upstairs, fell to my knees at the side of my bed and prayed, "Lord, I know that You are in control, that You love me and that You won't let anything touch me that isn't for my good and Your glory. I give You this mole to do with as you see fit. Just give me the strength to keep looking at you so I don't go down with the storm." The Lord brought peace to my heart.

A few days later at the grocery store I bent over to get a can of tomato soup and saw a new brown mole on my leg. The same panic overwhelmed me; my heart raced, my knees felt weak; I could barely breathe. I ran home, tears streaming down my face, and I bounded upstairs so that I could drop to my knees and pray.

Finally, after agonizing through a half a dozen new or different moles, I realized that God does not require that I be on my knees to talk to Him. I do not have to be in my bedroom. I can talk to him anytime, any place, and in any position.

The next time I found a new mole, I was driving. I looked in the rear-view mirror and saw a mole on the side of my neck. As the panic welled up within me, I gave it to the Lord and He delivered me from my fears.

Four years passed since my first surgery, during which time literally scores of moles were removed for biopsy.

As I watched the moles in question, some of them would change or get bigger. After watching them a month, I'd have Dr. Fitzpatrick look at them. Sometimes he said, "We'll keep watching this one," and other times he said, "We'd better check this one out."

I began to feel like a hypochondriac. One day Dr. Fitzpatrick checked several moles and removed three of them for biopsy.

"Dr. Fitzpatrick," I said, "I'm beginning to feel a little paranoid about these dumb moles. Are you sure I need to spend so much time concentrating on them?"

He had given an injection near a mole to deaden the pain and was waiting a few minutes for it to take effect.

"Well," he said, "we have three alternatives. We could stick our heads in the sand and pretend the disease of melanoma doesn't exist, or we could remove every last mole on your body. The reasonable thing, I think, is to do what we're doing. Be aware, and take action when indicated."

He cut out the mole and dropped it into a little jar and did the same with the other two moles. I took the jars to the hospital lab, and went back to work.

Dr. Fitzpatrick continued to remove moles for biopsy and, though it became routine, I experienced the human uneasiness of the unknown until I had received the "all clear." Increasingly, however, as I began to understand God's perfection in His dealings with me, confidence in Him erased my fears.

It had been about four years since my surgery, and so far all of the biopsies had shown the moles to be benign. I was beginning to feel hopeful and even optimistic about the future. My full-time work with cancer patients was going well, and I was thrilled to see how God was meeting needs.

Then one day as I worked at my desk at home the telephone rang. A woman said, "Is this Nell? Nell Collins? Just a moment, Dr. Fitzpatrick wants to talk to you."

I *knew* why he wanted to talk with me. When everything was okay, the nurse gave me the news. The only reason he would want to speak to me personally would be to tell me that the last biopsy had shown a malignancy.

This time, however, my response was opposite from the first time. I was not hysterical. I did not panic.

While waiting for Dr. Fitzpatrick to come to the telephone, I thought about a radio broadcast I had done a few days before for an overseas mission group. The interviewer asked, "What should a person do, how should a person react, when cancer is diagnosed?"

I answered, "If the person has truly become a child of God through faith in His Son, then that person can face any bad news by *living* Proverbs chapter three, verses five and six." Then I quoted those verses.

As I waited at my desk, I picked up a pen and wrote out those two verses in big letters on a scratch pad:

"TRUST IN THE LORD WITH ALL THINE HEART, AND LEAN NOT UNTO THINE OWN UNDERSTANDING.

"IN ALL THY WAYS ACKNOWLEDGE HIM, AND HE SHALL DIRECT THY PATHS."

Then I dropped to my knees beside my desk. "It's okay Lord," I prayed. "Whatever You want to do is okay with me. I'm Your child, and I want what You want."

At that moment, Dr. Fitzpatrick came on the telephone and said, "Nell, I suppose you have guessed why I need to talk with you. I'm afraid we have another melanoma."

My voice was steady, "What needs to be done?"

The peace I felt could only have come from God.

Again I had to wait a few days before being admitted to the hospital. Instead of crying and screaming, this time I squeezed into my schedule as many visits with cancer patients as I possibly could. A second malignancy is about the worst news a cancer patient can receive, yet I felt confident in the Lord's absolute perfection in dealing with me.

The night before my surgery I checked into the hospital, but before going to my room I stopped in to see two of my cancer patients who were also there for treatment. What a blessing it was to pray for each other and give each other emotional support.

When I got into the hospital bed that night, I felt the desire to write a letter to God, just to reaffirm my total trust in him. This letter has been an important part of my own life, because I return to it whenever I begin to concentrate on my problems instead of God's solutions. The letter also has helped many others in crisis to learn to actively continue to put confidence in the Lord:

Dear God,

Because I know You through faith in the Lord Jesus Christ, Your Word tells me that I belong to You as Your child (John 1:12).

I believe, according to Your Word, that You will do everything in my life for my eternal good and for Your glory (Rom. 8:28).

And so, because I trust You to be perfect in Your dealings with me, I make total surrender of my life to You (Rom. 12:1,2).

I give to You every personal desire that I have for my life. If You choose to give me the privileges of long life and good health, then I will use those gifts to honor Your name. I will not ask for those privileges unless You would see fit to give them to me for your glory (Ps. 31:15).

If You deem it wise to give me that which *seems* less than perfect to me, in my humanness, then it is my intent to trust You for those things that I cannot understand. I will thank You for working out Your plan for my life so that I will be conformed to the image of the precious Lord Jesus Christ. I will depend upon You to give me grace to always glorify You in the midst of *whatever* You choose for me (Rom. 8:29 and 2 Cor. 12:9).

It is my intent not to resent anything that You allow to come into my life, even when I can't see what You are intending for my tomorrows (Prov. 3:5,6).

Along with the apostle Paul, I would express before You my desire that Christ be magnified in my body, whe her by life or by death (Phil. 1:20, 21).

Lord Je us, I need You to keep me true to this

commitment and to show me immediately when I deviate from it (Ps. 139:23,24).

Because of Your perfect trustworthiness, I trust You completely (Ps. 18:30).

In Jesus' name. Amen.

Signed _____
Date _____

I had actually worked through all of the issues of the letter long before this second diagnosis hit, and the letter was simply a way of reaffirming my faith in God's goodness and sovereignty. It is vitally important for a person to establish this confidence *prior* to the time of crisis, because when trouble hits, it is often overwhelming. In the midst of an emergency, fear seems to prevent clear thinking and delay constructive action in the light of God's Word. But if the spiritual position has been established ahead of time, then it is far easier to simply *return* to that position by *reaffirming* it. Because this letter states clearly the reasons why I know I can trust God in any circumstance, I return to it again and again in times of trouble.

The malignant mole this time had appeared on my leg, and the skin for the graft was taken from the other leg. But when I woke up in the recovery room, the first things I saw were four Band-Aids on my arms!

"They found four more moles that they checked out," the nurse told me.

My heart sank, and a rebellious fist rose up inside me. *Am I going to have to be a mole-watcher for the rest of my life?* I thought angrily.

Immediately, however, I recognized this attitude as sin, and I repeated part of the prayer written to God:

"It is my intent not to resent *anything* that You allow to come into my life. . . ."

Later in the day I looked up, and who was walking into the recovery room but Sally Williams! She had taken off work and paid for a flight to Indianapolis to work as a special nurse for me after surgery for two days. Just having her there meant so much to me.

"We've got some good news," Sally said. "It appears that this melanoma is not metastatic." Metastasis occurs when cells break off from the original tumor and travel throughout the body establishing new tumors, making the disease much more difficult to fight.

"You mean it is a second primary?" I asked. Sally nodded joyfully. That meant the mole on my leg was totally unrelated to the one that had been on my back.

This time the graft "took" the first time, so my stay in the hospital was shorter. They sent me home on crutches, and soon I was back in full swing, visiting cancer patients more feverishly than ever.

XI

As the Lord showed me how to begin trusting Him on a moment-by-moment basis, He also showed me areas in my life where I lacked discipline and needed His help to change.

My life exhibited unorganized activity. I raced around the state, expending great amounts of energy but feeling frustrated with my chaotic schedule and vague priorities. I convoluted from crisis to crisis.

Getting arrested for speeding worried me constantly. Since I did not know how many weeks or months I had to live, and I needed, urgently, to see cancer patients across the state who were sick and dying and hysterical, I pushed the accelerator to the floor.

I drove hard and fast, on the lookout for the highway patrol because I was always speeding. My excuse: *I've got to get there fast. I've got see this cancer patient before it's too late. I'm doing the Lord's work. Surely God and the state police will understand.* The troopers, needless to say, were not at all impressed with my excuses for driving too fast.

I worked all day and half the night. Since I felt guilty about relaxing, I rarely took a scheduled day off. I asked people to pray for me, to pray for my emotional stability, never considering that I needed adequate sleep, rest, and relaxation to keep my mind stable.

I had always heard, "It's better to burn out than to rust

out," but the Lord was showing me that neither burning out nor rusting out are honor to Him. He wants us to live balanced, disciplined lives, quiet and efficient as a well-oiled machine, living responsibly before Him.

My apartment was always a mess. Not disciplined enough to pick up after myself or keep my apartment clean, I rarely entertained guests. Having company meant I'd have to break down and clean house, so I almost never invited anyone to my place.

My fingernails were always jagged and torn from my constant biting. Sometimes I tore the nail so far that my finger actually bled, leaving ugly, painful evidence of lack of self-discipline.

Most of the areas where I lacked discipline could be kept secret. Generally, people never knew that I was unorganized or that I exceeded the speed limit. No one knew whether I skipped devotions or if my personal prayer life went to zilch.

But one area that I couldn't hide, no matter what I did, was my lack of discipline in the area of eating. Oh, I could "pig out" in secret, and often did. But what I could not hide was the excess weight. Those extra pounds were like a neon light drawing attention to my lack of self-control.

When most people think about a cancer patient and weight, they think in terms of an uncontrolled weight *loss* caused by the cancer. In fact, many cancer patients live in fear of losing even an ounce, terrified that any weight loss might be the beginning of a long, downhill slide of "wasting away" to skin and bones. Sometimes an extreme weight loss is part of the process of cancer. It may be caused by the cancer itself or by treatment which affects the appetite.

Some cancer patients have the subconscious thought, *As long as I don't lose weight, I can't die with cancer.* Then he or she might eat like crazy to stay plump.

I wanted to "enjoy life." I knew that any day I could

wake up with a new lump or mole that would be the beginning of the end for me. *I might as well eat this chocolate cream pie*, I thought, *I may not be here next year to enjoy it.*

I knew that being a "junk food junkie" was unhealthy and that I should eat balanced, nutritious meals, but I couldn't seem to resist. God began convicting me about my undisciplined eating habits, but I continued to eat everything in sight.

Lillian, a woman in one of my supporting churches, helped me realize yet another area where I lacked discipline. Her spiritual maturity became a constant encouragement to me. She helped me sort out problems with different cancer patients, and often visited people for me when I could not go. She counseled with a deep understanding of the Word of God and a skill in using it. I shared with her some of my deeply personal concerns, including my frustration about my lack of discipline and my anguish about my family relationships. I had seen Mom several times since Daddy died, but the visits were short and infrequent. Mom didn't hesitate to chide me about it, and I resented her "bugging" me.

One time I was in the hospital for some routine tests, and Lillian came to visit me. After arranging my bedside table and pouring a glass of water for me, she sat down and looked directly at me.

"Nell," she said, "I know that your deepest desire is to be a good Christian and a good missionary." She paused, and I did not speak. "But before you can really accomplish that, God expects you to be a good daughter. The biblical principle is that you must honor your mother. Right now I'm afraid you have gotten so busy that you have cut her out of your life."

Leave it to Lillian to get right to the point. I told her about the note Mom had written me: "Guess I'll have to get cancer before you'll come and see me."

My heart felt heavy with guilt and I confessed to God

my part in the building of barriers between Mom and myself over the years.

As soon as I was released from the hospital I asked Mom to come to my apartment for a visit. I wanted to fix dinner for her and just talk. She was surprised at the invitation. Since she did not drive, I had to go out of town to pick her up, but Lillian had helped me realize that all my other work would be worthless if I did not do my part to repair my relationship with Mom.

On the way back to Indianapolis, I asked Mom's forgiveness for becoming too busy for her, and I told her that I loved her. I thanked her for being a mother who taught me the importance of God and the need for a spiritual value system.

Her response was simple and kind: "I just did the best I knew how, Nelia Anne."

I looked at Mom and saw a wonderful lady who had followed God in the best way she knew. Often I wondered how very different her life might have been from the day she had felt "called," if someone would have counseled her biblically. I wondered what our home might have been like if our family had had some teaching from the Bible on marriage and family living.

Because of this, I felt an ever-increasing desire that the counsel I gave people be not my opinion but God's Word. I knew it would be the only counsel with real and lasting benefit. Because of the problems I had seen in my own home, I knew it was vital to understand God's viewpoint in all areas of life, and to seek His perspective in every relationship, every decision, every problem, and every joy.

Whatever was in the past, I wanted to begin afresh with Mom, and this day marked a new understanding between us.

As I prayed about areas where I lacked discipline, God began showing me how to deal with them in *His* way.

When I left my hospital job to begin working full-time with cancer patients, I was visiting 100 cancer patients in the state of Indiana, most of them in the Indianapolis area. As I actively worked with these people—visiting in their homes or in the hospital, telephoning, writing notes, or sending reading materials—I believed with all my heart that I was the only person, maybe in the world, qualified to work with cancer patients the way I was doing it. I did not know of another person who was a registered nurse, a cancer patient, and a person with Bible college training. *Nobody,* I thought, *has been through what I've been through. I'm the only one who can do this work.*

I was thoroughly convinced and thoroughly convincing. Most people didn't argue the point with me. As a matter of fact, they agreed wholeheartedly.

The ministry mushroomed. Every day the referrals poured in, and nearly always the cancer patient was hysterical or the family members were overwhelmed by the crisis. Frequently the call to me came in the last desperate hours of the patient's life, and I would find myself chasing around from LaPorte to Vincennes, trying to see everybody who needed help.

Referrals began coming from other states. A friend of mine had her pilot's license, and she sometimes flew me to other cities to see people.

I worked eighteen hours a day, driving hundreds of miles most days, sometimes feeling overwhelmed by the tremendous needs. When I spoke at my supporting churches, I'd say, "Please pray for me. Pray that I'll have the wisdom to know which ones of the many people needing help I should see. So many people need help, and I can only see a few each day."

My paperwork became a nightmare. I prayed for help with it, and God led me to Margaret Chapman, a candid, articulate woman in her fifties. I first met Margaret when she was in the hospital, just before she went into surgery to have both breasts removed. She was deeply depressed and at the point of suicide. Margaret had worked for thirty years in government service, and her life had revolved around her career. Suddenly she faced cancer, the loss of her job, and a vast change in her financial status. She felt useless.

One night after her surgery she called me on the telephone, and we talked about her problems. On the telephone she prayed and trusted Christ as her personal Savior.

After a few weeks she expressed a desire to help out in some way with this ministry. She was recuperating from massive surgery and would never again be able to work away from home, but she needed something to do. At first she just typed a few letters. Later she was able to do more and more of my paperwork and eventually became my "right arm."

"For the first time in my life," I once heard her say, "I have real purpose to my life. Through all those years in government service, my life really had little meaning. But now I know that my life does have a purpose that is real and eternal, and I thank God for the cancer."

I thank God for this fine woman and the way she has given so generously of her time to help me. But even with her help, the ministry was growing so fast that soon we were both swamped with work.

The enormity of the cancer problem shocked me. It was difficult to comprehend how many millions of people all over the world have cancer now or will have it some day. The American Cancer Society predicts that in this country alone, one person in every four will have cancer eventually, and it will touch two out of three families. It was no wonder my telephone rang so often.

But when someone ventured, "Nell, you need people

to help you work with cancer patients," I would shake my head.

"You can't relate to a cancer patient unless you've had cancer," I would say, ending the discussion.

During this time, Mary Beth Moster wrote *Living With Cancer* (Moody Press), a handbook for cancer patients and their families. The book described this ministry with cancer patients in some detail. As a result of reading *Living With Cancer*, people all over the country began calling me to speak in churches, at missions conferences, at women's retreats, and at Christian colleges. Though I thanked God for making it possible for me to minister in a greater geographical area, my schedule became more and more frenzied.

God blessed the ministry mightily. Many people came to know the Lord and it was exciting to see those who had been terrified of cancer and all its implications begin to face the unknown future with peace and serenity. But I began to realize that there was only one of me and millions of cancer patients.

As I was leaving my office at the church one day, one of the board members stopped me on the steps.

"Nell," he said, "I want to talk with you a minute." He cleared his throat a couple of times and avoided looking at me.

"You know, Nell," he began, "your case load is getting out of control. I'm worried that one person can't give these people what they need. Nobody can do it all. Nobody could visit all those people in any meaningful way."

I defended myself, using the same arguments I had used for years. "Nobody has had the experiences that I've had. Nobody's been through what I've been through. If you haven't experienced it personally, how can you understand what people with cancer are facing? If you haven't had cancer and combined it with nursing and Bible college, you just can't do it . . ."

"Okay, okay," he said, laughing a little. "I see your point. But I just want you to consider 2 Timothy."

He flipped open his Bible, and the verse stood out as if it were in boldface type.

"And the things that thou hast heard of me among many witnesses, the same commit thou to faithful men, *who shall be able to teach others also*" (2 Timothy 2:2, emphasis mine).

"You'll just have to deal with that verse, Nell."

Without another word he walked to his car and drove off. I stood there on the steps, my face red, my eyes full of tears, anger welling up inside of me.

He was right. Of course he was right. How could I have been so wrong to believe that I was the only one God could use for this ministry? I realized my sin and confessed it to God.

I thought about Eddie and Margie and the beautiful friendship we had been able to develop, simply because I was able to spend *time* with them. My heart ached for the families in crisis who would love to have a friend who lived in the same town, who could spend time with them, and who could be there when needed. What a wonderful thing to have a friend who could consistently bring hope in the midst of crisis.

Certainly there were "faithful men" (and women!) in communities all over the country. Perhaps I could entrust to them the things the Lord was teaching me, and they could then teach others—the cancer patients in their communities.

It took several more months of prayer and soul-searching to know how I should go about finding those faithful men and women. Eventually God showed me the way.

Every day I received calls from Christian people who were members of fundamentally sound, Bible-teaching churches. Every day believers were calling to see if I would visit their neighbors, mothers-in-law, cousins, aunts, uncles, and grandmothers. They expressed a sincere desire to see their loved ones "come to Christ" or "get back into fellowship with the Lord."

It would always be something like this: "Nell, will you go see my uncle? *I don't know what to do!*"

I finally realized that there are many people who can minister to cancer patients in crisis. It is not necessary for them to have had cancer. It is not necessary to have been a nurse or to have trained in Bible college. It is only necessary to know the Lord and to have received His comfort during any kind of trouble. I recalled the verse that had meant so much to me when I had first gone into this work:

"Blessed be God, even the Father of our Lord Jesus Christ, the Father of mercies, and the God of all comfort, Who comforteth us in *all our tribulation,* that we may be able to comfort them which are in *any* trouble by the comfort with which we ourselves are comforted of God" (2 Corinthians 1:3,4—emphasis mine).

It does not matter what kind of "affliction," or trouble, we have endured. If we have been comforted by God at *any* time, during *any* kind of difficulty, then we can comfort others!

That same passage continues with a wonderful thought:

"For as the sufferings of Christ abound in us, so our consolation also aboundeth by Christ. And *whether we be afflicted, it is for your consolation and salvation.*" (vs. 5,6—emphasis mine).

As I prayed and studied the Word, God began giving me a plan. He even gave me the name: *Hope in Crisis.* That name is the crux of this expanded ministry. It brings hope to people in the midst of crisis.

It was exciting, venturing out into this new concept of ministry. Since I had personally worked with many hundreds of people, I knew that *Hope in Crisis* had to be first, last, and always, a ministry devoted to meeting the *spiritual* needs of cancer patients, for it is only through spiritual strength that physical and emotional crises can be met.

Hope in Crisis would need to give support based on the love of Jesus Christ. It would be friend-to-friend communication of biblical alternatives to human distresses.

Hope in Crisis workers would be members of local Bible-believing churches who would work under the authority of the pastor and under the administration of a coordinator from that church.

Through *Hope in Crisis* more people would become involved in the ministry, and many more cancer patients would be helped.

For several months prior to the development of *Hope in Crisis,* I felt "in limbo" as far as my own cancer treatment was concerned. Since I'd had melanoma twice already, I was at high risk to get melanoma again.

One day I was seeing one of my doctors for a routine physical checkup. He talked with me about being responsible in decision-making. As a Christian, he emphasized that God expects responsible behavior.

"But I'm so confused," I said. "People are giving me all kinds of conflicting advice. Some people tell me I should go on Laetrile, but that it is illegal and expensive. Most medical people say it doesn't work anyway. Other people tell me I should drink herbs and go on a special diet. I'm scared of chemotherapy, because sometimes people get so sick from it. I just don't know what I should do, if anything."

"Nell," he said, "you really need to equip yourself with some factual information. Cancer chemotherapy is not my field, but you should talk with a chemotherapy specialist. A specialist can advise you about whether or not further treatment is needed."

"I don't want to even talk to a chemotherapy specialist. I can't stand the thought of taking a drug."

"Well," he said slowly, "I want you to pray about it. You *will* pray about it, won't you?"

That's not fair, I thought glumly. *How can a missionary nurse refuse to pray about something?*

My response showed a limited understanding of chemotherapy. My attitude had always been: *No drugs. I'd rather die than go on drugs.* But I agreed to pray about it.

Not long after that, I was in the hospital having some tests. I agreed at least to talk with Dr. Adams, the chemotherapy specialist.

He came into my room, examining my chart. After talking at length about my history, he spelled it out.

"Nell," he said, "I'd like to see you on a two-year program of immunotherapy. Immunotherapy, as you know, is not chemotherapy. Chemotherapy works directly on the cells to either destroy the cancer cells or make them unable to reproduce. Immunotherapy, on the other hand, builds up the body's own immune system to fight the cancer with the body's natural defense mechanisms.

"Immunotherapy doesn't really 'immunize' you. But if there are any stray tumor cells in your body, your own immune system is alerted, Paul Revere style, to gear up and seek and kill those enemy cells."

He explained that there are several theories about why some people get cancer and others do not. Many experts agree that the body's own immune system may be a key to fighting cancer, and this is the basic premise of immunotherapy.

"I want to make it clear to you," he continued, "that this is an experimental program. We don't know if it will work or not. We really have no way of knowing if there are any stray tumor cells in your body. But if there are, immunotherapy is the most effective method we now have to fight them."

After praying about it some more, I became convinced that the immunotherapy program made sense to me, with my kind of cancer, and with my history of two primary melanomas. It would not necessarily be right or recommended for every cancer patient. But in my case I believed that the responsible thing to do was to give it a try.

Going through the immunotherapy program, for me, was like going to "language school." Although there are definite differences between immunotherapy and chemotherapy, I began to more fully understand the questions, problems, and confusions about the drugs used in the treatment of cancer. This understanding opened a new line of communication with "my people," and God blessed it in many ways.

My immunotherapy involved going to Dr. Adams' office once a month for two years. The nurse would lead me to an office in the back where she would pour a vial of clear liquid into a glass of Tang or Diet Pepsi. I drank it down and that was that.

In the course of this two year period, I began putting on weight, lots of weight. I had always been overweight, so at first I didn't pay much attention. Like any other cancer patient, I rationalized, "Well, at least I'm not wasting away."

The nurses in Dr. Adams' office weighed me when I went in for my immunotherapy drug. One day the scale tipped at 230 pounds.

When I saw Dr. Adams I said, "This drug is making me fat! What is in it? I'm gaining weight like crazy and it has to be the drug."

Dr. Adams studied my chart in his calm, easygoing manner.

"Nell," he said, "there is nothing in that drug that would cause you to gain weight. Your body might be all revved up to fight cancer cells, therefore making you feel better and giving you a better appetite. But if you are gaining weight, it's because you're eating too much."

Some nerve, I thought, as I waddled out of his office. Then I wondered, *Could it be true?* Could I be responsible for my own fatness?

XII

I drove around in the parking lot for fifteen solid minutes, hoping that somebody would leave and I could get a parking space closer to the hospital. This parking lot sprawled for acres, and I secretly dreaded visiting patients here.

Finally I gave up and parked in a space that seemed a mile from the hospital.

I dropped some papers on the floor on the passenger side of the car. Leaning over, I saw quickly that there was no way I could pick them up. I couldn't ever wear shoes that tied because I couldn't bend over to reach the laces. The papers would have to stay on the floor. Even getting out of the car and into a standing position required a major effort. I huffed and puffed and lugged my 230 pounds across the lot. My self-esteem dragged on the ground behind me.

The night before I had given a program for one of my supporting churches, and gave the premiere showing of a film which was made to describe the ministry with cancer patients. We set up the screen and turned out the lights, and everybody's attention focused on Nell Collins, the Blimp.

Rolls upon rolls of fat and all three chins were displayed in living color. The black dress I had thought so flattering looked like it would fit Jonah's whale.

When I got up to speak to the group I could barely force out the words. *How can I tell these ladies anything? They've all got more on the ball than I do. They all have their lives under control, and I'm an undisciplined, unorganized, fat slob.*

The film also showed my fingernails, which were jagged and torn, chewed down past the quick. Since I talk with my hands, those jagged nails waved around for all to see.

Several days later i was having a routine physical with the same doctor who had insisted that I pray about seeing a chemotherapy specialist. He looked me right in the eye and said, "Nell, your eating habits are out of control. You are blaming this weight gain on your immunotherapy, but you are going to have to face the fact that you are responsible for what goes into your mouth. How can you expect people to have victory over their fear of cancer if you don't allow God to give *you* victory over your fork?"

A terrible pain pierced my heart, and I bit my lip to keep from crying.

He was right, of course, but I was furious with him for being so honest.

Like most overweight people, I had plenty of excuses. Though some people will not admit that they overeat ("It's glandular"), I knew that I ate too much, too often, and all the wrong things. *I've always been this way,* I thought. *I just can't help it.*

I'm a foodaholic, I thought. *My eating habits are totally out of control.* I felt as helpless to change as an alcoholic or drug addict might feel.

Eating is my greatest pleasure in life, I realized. *Whether Big Macs, Twinkies, or burritos from Taco Bell. I love them. I love them all.*

No matter how pleasantly or terribly my day is going, I respond to it by eating. When happy, I celebrate by eating. When sad, I pull myself out of it by eating. When with people, I socialize by eating. When all alone and blue, I want to make myself feel better by eating.

I agonized at the very thought of going on another diet.

Losing weight, in itself, is no terrific accomplishment. In my lifetime I have lost *hundreds* of pounds, only to put them right back on again.

It has been a roller coaster ride. Up and down. Down and up. Taking it off. Putting it on. I would be fat, so I'd go on a starvation diet. I might lose some pounds, but always I'd slip back into my old habit patterns and get fat again. Then I'd feel so guilty about not being able to control myself that I'd eat even more. Finally I'd get so sick of being fat that I'd plunge into another starvation diet. Because I was always fat, I was always dieting.

One of my wilder diets consisted of 400 calories per day. What I figured I could eat each day was:

1 piece Kentucky Fried Chicken
1 container cole slaw
2 dill pickles

Every afternoon I would visit the Kentucky Colonel and have my pickles and chicken.

I did lose weight.

After being on that diet a while, I started going to a health club with a friend to exercise. However, on the way home we would stop by the Dairy Queen and get a hot fudge sundae with nuts, whipped cream, and a cherry on top.

My emotions went up and down with my eating. When I was eating chicken and pickles, I was happy because I was on my diet. When I was eating a sundae I was discouraged because I was off my diet.

Though it took me years to be able to admit it, I finally realized that I was not dealing with the real issue. My problem was not being fat: my problem was *lack* of self-discipline.

As a missionary, I had a built-in excuse. I was frequently invited to people's homes, and those dear folks always provided the most delicious and wonderful meals. "How can I refuse another helping of roast beef? Noodles? Oh, yes, I'd love some more. Cherry pie? Well, just a smidge."

Church carry-in suppers were the best of all. It just seemed that food and fellowship went together. As I heaped up my plate with the casseroles, fried chicken, and rich homemade desserts, it never failed that someone would say, "Now, pastor, let's not have any preaching on gluttony!" And everyone would chuckle as we all piled on more food.

It occurred to me that gluttony is the one sin that Christians joke about. We are very serious about lust and drunkenness and stealing, then we turn around and laugh about "pigging out."

When I went to the Word for direction in this area, it surprised me that the Bible said so *much* about gluttony.

When I looked up these verses, they spoke to my heart.

Proverbs 23:1—Eating requires diligent consideration of the available foods. Observe what is there, and learn to make choices. *Think about* and *plan* what you are going to eat.

Ecclesiastes 6:7—The appetite of the flesh cannot be satisified. True satisfaction does not come in a Dunkin' Donuts box.

Proverbs 25:16—Eat to *sufficiency*, not to capacity.

1 Peter 4:3—"Pigging out" is an *old nature* lifestyle. Gluttony is as wrong as any other sin.

Deuteronomy 21:20—Gluttony is a sin of rebellion.

The Word showed me clearly that weight control is a matter of spiritual importance and value. How I eat shows my confidence in God's plan for my life.

Eating appropriately shows respect for my body, which is God's creation and residence. It also reveals my personal commitment to God. If I have given my body as a living sacrifice (Rom. 12:1,2), then I must make choices under God's control and for His glory.

What it gets down to is this:

PLEASING GOD FIRST,
WHETHER I FEEL LIKE IT OR NOT

Pleasing God First is a matter of living *responsibly*, making choices based not on desires, but on the Word of God. *We do not have to be slaves to our desires.*

Facing my responsibility meant that I no longer could blame other people, or my circumstances, for my fatness. It was easy for me to blame my childhood experiences and my immunotherapy.

I thought, *If only people hadn't fed me so much macaroni and cheese and given me boxes of cookies to keep me quiet when I was little. I know I overeat, but that's the way I was conditioned as a child. I can't help it. It must be the immunotherapy drug. I can't help it.*

What I was doing, of course, was blame-shifting. In the same way that Adam blamed Eve and Eve blamed the serpent, I blamed my childhood experiences for something that was my responsibility. Though habits are established in childhood, we *can* break the pattern! God has created us in His image, for His glory. Old habit patterns CAN BE CHANGED as we live in obedience to His Word.

Kathy, a woman in one of my supporting churches in another town, was keenly aware of physical fitness. She helped me work out a systematic program that would increase my physical activity while I decreased my calorie intake. I started gradually, walking briskly only five minutes a day. As my weight came off, I increased my walking time to 30-40 minutes a day.

Later, Kathy believed the Lord was leading her to become a nurse, so she came to Indianapolis and enrolled in practical nursing school. She needed a place to live while in school, so we shared an apartment. She encouraged me in my exercise program, and we began to play tennis, ride bikes, ski and jog. It has been a thrill for me to participate in physical activities I'd always been too fat to enjoy.

I learned to discipline my intake of food.

Each day's supply of calories would be like money in the checking account. When I "withdraw" calories from my day's allotment, I immediately write it down in the same way that I record and deduct the checks that I write. I write down the *type* of food, the *amount* of food, the *caloric* value, and the *time* of day. Accustomed to nibbling all day long, I knew that I had to discipline the frequency of eating.

My whole life I had stashed Ding-Dongs and candy bars in the cupboard. Then I read:

"Put ye on the Lord Jesus Christ and *make not provision for the flesh to fulfil the lusts thereof*" (Romans 13:14—emphasis mine).

Could it be that I had been *lusting* for chocolate cake and ice cream? I cleared all the junk food out of my apartment so I would not make *provision for the flesh*.

After I had been on my new eating program for a few days I spoke again at a church and showed the film. This time, however, it didn't depress me, and I didn't feel inferior. I *looked* exactly the same, but I felt better about myself because I knew that I was *doing* what God wanted me to do, even if it didn't show yet.

It took two whole years to lose 95 pounds, and in the process there were days when I failed, went on eating binges, and felt like giving up. I found it crucial for me to admit my sin immediately before God, then get right back on the program without wallowing in self-pity or self-condemnation.

Losing a tremendous amount of weight does require some mental adjustments. I walk by a window and think my reflection is someone else. People I have known for years do not recognize me, and I have to re-introduce myself to them. I had learned to dress and sit and walk like a fat person. It now takes much less push to get up and sit down, and it takes a different amount of thrust to walk. I sit in less of the pew at church. My Volkswagen would have been too small last year. I literally would not have been able to get into it. Now there is room to spare. It has taken some adjusting, but it is worth it.

During this same period of time the Lord began showing me how to get my *life* in control in areas in addition to eating.

Many of my problems with lack of discipline involved my use of *time*. I didn't plan or schedule anything, so I was usually in a state of panic with far more to do than anyone could get done.

God began to show me the value of *writing things down*, planning for the month, the week, and the day. I scheduled time with patients and with *Hope in Crisis* teams and coordinators, but I allowed enough flexibility to be able to go to people in real emergencies. I established priority criteria so that I wouldn't always be in a quandary over which patient to see on a particular day. I scheduled time to clean my house, do my laundry, exercise, and sleep. I began to allow enough time to drive to my destinations so that I wouldn't always be running late, and this, in itself, reduced the temptation to exceed the speed limit. Because I stopped being so harried and rushed, I also stopped biting my nails.

All of these changes took place in my life *gradually*, and I still occasionally slip back into my old unstructured habit patterns. But now I recognize that a chaotic life does not honor the Lord, and what is not honoring to Him is sin. When I fail, I immediately confess it to God, accept His forgiveness and pray for His power and His control, for it is only through Him that change is possible.

My weight loss has added a new and unexpected dimension to my ministry. As I have spoken in churches or women's groups, I have been swamped with questions, not always about cancer, but sometimes about my weight loss.

"How did you do it?" they have wanted to know.

So many people have asked me this question that I have realized that many other people have struggled with out-of-control eating habits. The Lord has shown me that I must not ignore the needs of these people just because they have not had cancer. Lack of self-discipline in any area can lead to great crisis in people's lives.

In time I started giving weight-control clinics in my supporting churches. The response has been great, weight has been lost, and people have found that God will give His control, even in the area of eating.

Not long ago, I saw a friend I hadn't seen in years, but I didn't recognize her because she had gained so much weight. She came up to me and introduced herself; we chatted a bit, and she said she would write me. A few weeks later I received this letter:

Dear Nellie,

Well, I finally am writing—did you give up on me?

Nellie—I really don't know where to begin—I have been saved not quite eight years.

I feel like my life is going nowhere. I have blue periods and when I'm in one of those, I think *awful* things about myself! I do not have the joy Jesus promised me—I want to leave this world and go Home to be with Him. I realize this is wrong because God tells us to "occupy til I return." I let life upset me—I mean when trials come my way, I let them get me down. I realize this is wrong because it does not present a good testimony to the unsaved. I feel as if I've turned my family from God and that they'll never be saved! (I pray that's not true!)

I get discouraged so easily. I live alone and I know Satan uses that to his advantage. Nellie, I feel like there is no use in keeping on trying—I have failed so often.

Nellie, I feel like the Christian life didn't work for me! I realize I can't see into the minds and lives of other Christians, but they seem so happy. I realize I shouldn't look at others, but only Jesus. I am so sad usually, not always tho!

I *do* want my life to please and honor the Lord, but I don't feel it does. I am not happy at my work, but I've been trying to ask God to help me. I am a Christian and a nurse and all I seem to do is add to the hurt of the world! I am so discontented, Nellie. I feel as if God isn't working in my life.

I don't know if you'll feel like answering me, but at least you know how I feel!

There are other things I would tell you—maybe in another letter.

Love and prayers,
Phyllis

My heart went out to Phyllis. I did know how she felt; I had been there so many times! Again I saw the pattern— people have problems, but God has solutions!

I went to see her as soon as I could. We chatted about her letter and I told her that I would like to help in any way I could. She told me that her weight had been up to 307 pounds, that she had lost 38 pounds and gained half of it back. Her weight was now 285.

Then she looked down at the floor and cried.

"The more I talk to you, Nellie, the more depressed I get. You're so *vital*—I feel that life has passed me by. I'm not a good Christian, I'm not a good nurse, and I don't have a willing spirit to change."

I showed Phyllis my picture at 230 pounds. "When they took that picture for my driver's license, my life was out of control. I couldn't have helped you then because I couldn't help myself. Now you say I can't help you because I'm too vital and I depress you!" I smiled and paused a moment. "No one could have helped me either, Phyllis. I had to turn to God and His Word for help."

Phyllis was not a cancer patient, but her *crisis* was just as real. I counseled her in exactly the same way I had counseled hundreds of people in crisis!

I took a piece of paper and drew a sketch of a Bible:

What I was      What God wants me to be.

"We get from 'what I was,'" I told Phyllis, "to 'what God wants me to be' by being *transformed*, and the Bible tells us exactly how we can be transformed."

I showed her Romans 12:1 and 2:

"I beseech you therefore, brethren, by the mercies of God, that you present your bodies a living sacrifice, holy, acceptable unto God, which is your reasonable service. And be not conformed to this world, but be ye transformed by the renewing of your mind. . . ."

I looked squarely at Phyllis. "Vitality comes from the Word of God. The word 'transformed' means metamorphosis, which is a mysterious, beautiful change. It is *metamorphosis* that changes a caterpillar into a butterfly, and it is God's transformation that changes lives. It is God who changes the caterpillar, and it is God who is changing me."

"But, Nellie, you seem to have it all together. I can't stop eating."

"Phyllis, to say 'I can't' is cheapening God's provision. He has given us the Holy Spirit, who gives us *power* to do what's right. Now don't get the idea that I'm perfect. I'm not. God still has a lot of work to do with me, but *He is* changing me! I praise Him for giving me self-control in the area of eating. He has also given me self-discipline in other areas. I no longer drive like a madman, watching for cops out the rear-view mirror. I don't chew my nails any more. I keep my house clean, upstairs and down. I'm doing a better job of scheduling, and I plan time to relax in order to keep my mind stable. I ride my bike and play tennis.

"All of this is evidence of *God's transforming power,* and it is available to *you!*"

XIII

It was a hurt deep inside, a sadness I had not experienced at any other time in my life.

A sweet fragrance filled the air from baskets of fresh-cut flowers.

Seeing all the people there brought more tears, but I tried to compose myself before entering the room. I had been to more funerals than I cared to count. Many of my cancer patients had become my dear friends, and some of them had gone on to be with the Lord. I had cried at their funerals, too.

But this time it was different. This time it was my mother.

I never dreamed that it would be so painful to lose her.

During the last few years, Mom had been terribly ill. Her diabetes had gone out of control; she had to have both legs amputated. Her heart had been damaged by the diabetic condition, and it simply could not pump the needed oxygen, so her lungs were also affected. Many times she was unable to breathe except in short, labored gasps.

Mom and I became very close after that first time I made a real effort to 'honor my mother.' I had asked her to forgive he many times I had disappointed her as a rebellious young person, and she asked me to forgive her shortcomings as a ˌother.

I was able to thank her for loving me, for raising me in such a way that I eventually would be able to make a commitment to Jesus Christ. She had instilled in me a spiritual value system that enabled me to know that only God could meet the needs of my heart. I shared with her how much I appreciated the qualities of her character that influenced my life, primarily her steadfast faithfulness and her unconditional love for me, even when I was breaking her heart.

In the last months she had been hospitalized again and again, suffering one crisis after another.

Mom did not see me as a "counselor." I was her little girl. We still had differences of opinion about many things, but we had come to an acceptance of one another, and on that basis we were able to work together through the same Bible study I had prepared for cancer patients. Mom did not have cancer, but she was in physical crisis and she, too, had to choose between being consumed with her physical problems or God's solutions to those problems.

My heart ached to see her suffer; to see her in such pain was agony for me. I felt so helpless watching her fight her final battle.

One day in the hospital, I turned on the radio, and a familiar melody filled the room: "Amazing Grace, how sweet the sound . . ."

"God does give us grace to endure even this, Nelia Ann," she whispered.

Now she is gone, and so is a big part of my life. But something beautiful happened between us in those last dark months, and I thank God for the blessing of our time together.

As I left the memorial service and stepped out into the blazing spring sunlight, I thought of the irony. Ten years ago, when my cancer was first diagnosed, my greatest fear was that Mom would not be able to bear seeing me suffer and die. Instead, it was Mom who suffered, but those years we had together to mend our relationship were precious to me, and I will always treasure them.

Not long after Mom's funeral, I got a call about Karen Johnson. I had first seen Karen a number of years before in a local hospital. I remembered vividly that first visit with her. She had stretched out on her hospital bed, lying on her back. A bandage on her leg had bulged under the white sheet, and she had been engrossed in a paperback novel when I quietly entered the room.

I had tapped lightly on the door so I wouldn't startle her. "Hi," I had said, "I'm Nell." She had looked up at me, obviously wondering what I was doing there.

"Your friend Diane Bond asked me to stop by to see you."

The day before, Diane had told me about Karen. "She's a single gal," Diane had said, "A few years older than you. *She had a malignant melanoma on her leg.*"

The words had hit me like a club. Even though I had been counseling cancer patients for several years, it still gave me a queasy feeling to see someone with malignant melanoma—my kind of cancer.

Karen hadn't looked overly delighted to see me, but she said, "Come on in and sit down. Sorry I can't get up."

We had chatted a moment, then I said, "Hey, did Diane tell you that I had melanoma surgery on my back a few years ago?"

Suddenly she had become very interested and wanted to hear all about how I'd done. To see me alive and well had no doubt encouraged her.

"The only thing, Nell," she had said, "is that mine went deeper than yours. I knew that mole was there for a long time. Guess I should've gone to the doctor sooner. Oh, well. They think I'll make it okay. I'm going to have chemotherapy, but I'll be able to go back to work in a couple of weeks. I won't let this thing get me down, though. I'll go back to work and forget all of this." She waved her arm indicating the hospital and the cancer.

Karen reminded me of many other cancer patients I had come to know. Unable to deal with the reality of the situation, they shove it "underground" in their minds, acting as though the cancer never happened. Though it is possible to dwell on the cancer too much, I believe that we should face cancer or any problem in life as an opportunity to adjust our lives and use the problem to God's glory and for His purposes.

Karen, however, had seen the cancer only as an interference in her daily routine. She had confined the conversation purely to her physical problems, and I stayed only a few moments that day.

When Karen started through chemotherapy a few days later, she had gritted her teeth and endured the chemotherapy and the nausea that followed with the sheer power of her will.

We had met regularly in her home or in my office. We could talk about spiritual matters in only the most general way, but I remained her friend.

Karen had gone back to work, convinced that they had "taken care of the cancer." We had stayed in touch and went out to lunch together fairly often. She seemed to like me, but she had resisted opening up with me.

For four years we continued on this basis. I saw hundreds of other cancer patients, but I never lost track of Karen. Even though she had her cancer filed away in her mind under "Bad Memories—Keep Out" I knew that she had a high risk for the melanoma to become metastatic. I also knew that she didn't have the spiritual resources to deal with that kind of trauma if it happened.

One day not long after Mom's funeral, I got another call from Diane. "Karen found a mole in her eyelid, Nell," she said, "and biopsy showed it to be more cancer. X-ray revealed another one in her lung and she's gone to another state to have it removed."

Knees weak and mouth dry, I said, "Thanks for calling, Diane. I'll be in touch."

Whenever I hear bad news about one of my patients, I feel the trauma of it, as though it were happening to me. But with Karen I knew it really could happen to me in just that same way. I could identify the waves of panic as they began to well up within me.

"Dear God," I said, affirming again the prayer I had written to Him years before and by now knew by heart, "Because I know You through faith in the Lord Jesus Christ, Your Word tells me that I belong to You as Your child . . . I make total surrender of my life to You . . . I give to You every personal desire that I have for my life . . . I will depend upon You to give me the grace to always glorify You in the midst of *whatever* You choose for me . . . It is my intent not to resent anything that You allow to come into my life . . . Because of Your perfect trustworthiness I trust You completely. In Jesus' name, Amen."

Just praying that prayer once again helped me focus on eternal values, and God gave me peace in my heart. I knew that I couldn't help Karen if I weren't totally trusting the Lord myself.

When Karen returned home from out of state, I called and asked if I could bring her some lunch.

She sat up in her hospital bed in the living room of her apartment. I opened the McDonald's sack and arranged her lunch on the bed tray. She didn't object when I asked if I could say grace. That was the first time she had allowed me to pray in her presence.

She looked up at me and said, "Nell, I'm going to lick this thing . . . I won't let it get the best of me." Tough. Determined. A real fighter. But then she showed me the three new places which had popped up since her recent surgery. They were just like little marbles under the skin. The original tumor had been on her leg four years before, but at least one tumor cell had escaped removal by surgery and missed destruction by the chemotherapy that followed. That cell "laid low" for a while, biding its time for weeks, months, years. Now Karen's time bomb had exploded.

Sipping my iced tea, I said, "Karen, I'm just wondering something. I'm wondering if you feel like I can't really understand what you're going through? I mean it's been ten years since my first surgery, and even though I had another primary melanoma, I haven't had metastasis. In that sense I can't *really* know. But I can try to understand how I would feel if I were going through it. Even though time is on my side, it wouldn't be impossible for me to have a metastatic recurrence. That possibility will be with me for the rest of my life. So I can imagine how I would react if it did happen to me."

She looked at me intently.

"To tell you the absolute truth, Karen, I couldn't begin to handle what you are going through, if it weren't for the Lord. He is the One who gives me the strength to face things like this."

I stayed close to Karen over the next several weeks, and agonized with her as each new lump appeared. The melanoma was rampant, out of control, and the treatments weren't stopping it.

One night she called me in tears. "Oh, Nell," she said, "it hurts so bad." It was the first time she had expressed any emotion to me.

"Are you taking the pain pills they gave you?"

"Yes, but they're not helping."

"Listen, I'll call the doctor for you. Maybe they can give you something that works better."

The doctor decided that she needed to go back into the hospital, so the next day I saw her there and she was resting more comfortably.

She showed me her latest knot, a huge black, egg-shaped lump sticking out of her shin bone.

I sat down beside her bed and took her hand. "Karen, I've been your friend for a long time. We've been through a lot together. I just want you to know that I really do care about you." Tears filled my eyes.

"Oh, Nell, I'm at the end of myself. I can't handle this any more. I do need God."

What an unspeakable privilege it was to be able to simply show my friend that Jesus Christ is the Way, the Truth, and the Life. And though she lived only twelve days after her decision to receive Jesus Christ as her own Savior, she had a peace and confidence that only comes from God. This newfound peace was obvious to friends and family as they saw her changed attitude.

A few days after Karen's funeral, I was riding in a car to speak at a ladies' missionary meeting when I leaned over to adjust the strap on my shoe. My heart skipped a beat as I noticed a bump the size of a nickel on my leg. *Just like Karen's!* I thought.

A tidal wave of panic hit as I remembered what had happened to Karen and realized that it might have happened to me also.

I thought about Jesus in the Garden of Gethsemane, when He prayed about the painful crucifixion He faced, and I prayed as He did, "Father, if it is Your will, let this cup pass from me. *Nevertheless . . ."*

I stopped a moment. It was the *nevertheless* that made the difference between peace and panic. It was the *nevertheless* that revealed that my trust would be in God's perfect plan to use me in whatever way He chose.

"*Nevertheless,* not my will but thine be done."

Once again, I began to see that God could use something which seemed terrible in my life to demonstrate to others that no human distress is so great that He can't bring good out of it.

I went to see Ruth, one of my patients who also happened to have had melanoma. When I showed her the bump on my leg, she became very frightened.

"Oh, Nell," she cried. "I love the Lord, I really do, but I'm so scared."

"You know, Ruth, since I had my first diagnosis ten years ago, I've hardly had a month go by without some kind of mole or lump or bump or even a new pain coming up. It is a constant matter of putting out brush fires, of meeting scary things head on *through the Lord*."

"I guess," Ruth said, "that I haven't really learned to do that yet."

"What I've discovered, Ruth, is that it is a *way of life*. We never know what we'll find up ahead, in the next bend of the road. We might have to face some humanly scary and unpleasant things. But *no matter what*, we can know that God is sovereign, He makes no mistakes, and He is in control. That is why we can have peace and confidence, in the midst of trouble as we trust Him wholly. Problems come every day; some are small, and some are huge. But God's solutions are constant, never-changing. When we are insulated by His Words, He gives us great security."

Later that day, as I met with other patients, it was wonderful to share with them how God had met me at the point of my need and calmed my fears. I met with my *Hope in Crisis* coordinators and other workers, and one of them said, "Nell, I'm praying specifically that it will be just a plain old harmless bump."

"Well," I said, "I appreciate that, and I do want you to pray. But please join me in praying for God's perfect will, not my imperfect wish. It may be that He can use my life best by my suffering and eventual death, and if so, then that's what I want, too. That is real freedom, because if I'm living in God's economy, nothing can get me down."

During the 48 hours I had to wait for the results of the

tests they took on that bump, God gave me peace that could only come from Him. I calmly considered the realities of what I might have to face: *If I can't drive my car with a clutch, I'll need to trade cars. My insurance should be okay for awhile. If I can't climb stairs, I can move my bedroom downstairs.* Even though all of these practical considerations were real concerns, the overriding fact was that my deepest desire was that God's perfect will be done. *No matter what.*

I called the doctor, and this time he talked to me personally, so he must have had more than the usual concern. "It looks like your bump is just a spur on the bone, Nell. It's not malignant! I'm sorry you had to wait even a day to get the results."

"Well, Dr. Adams," I said, "I don't know what the future holds for me, but I thank the Lord for whatever it is." As I hung up, I also thanked God for the fine doctors who take a personal interest in their patients.

A few days later I was sitting at my desk, catching up on some paperwork. I had received a letter from Karen's nephew, and as I read it my heart warmed with the encouragement he gave me.

Nell,

I would like to take this opportunity to thank you from the bottom of my heart for the help and support you have given to both my family and my aunt. When I think of God working through you to reach Aunt Karen, and her accepting Jesus, tears of joy fill my eyes. There are not enough English words in my vocabulary to justly show my warm appreciation for your courage and the testimony you share with so many in need. . . .

As I was reading the letter, the telephone rang.

"Nell?" a shaken voice asked. "This is Janice Allen."

I had been seeing Janice's father for several weeks. *Wonder what's wrong?* I thought.

Before I had time to ask the question, Janice continued, "My Dad is back in the hospital, and he's so blue . . . I told him I'd call you, 'cause you're the 'Blues Lady!' "

I chuckled with her in a sweet, family-like closeness that allows a sense of humor even during difficult days.

"He doesn't want any visitors," she continued, "but he wants to see you. He keeps asking for you. Can you come?"

"Be right there," I said, grabbing my purse and sweater.

As I drove to the hospital I thought of the wonderful privilege God has given me to share His Son with those in need. I also thought about the preciousness of life and how I treasure each day He has given me.

How good is the Lord, I thought. *At 29 I thought I wouldn't live to be 30, and He has given me more than a decade beyond that. The future is unknown to me I don't know what it will bring. Will my time bomb of melanoma explode? Or will I have a long life? I don't know. I may have to walk through "the valley of the shadow" many times, but because of Jesus, the valley is bright. Whatever happens, I know that God is in control, and I can trust Him completely.*

ABOUT THE AUTHORS

Nell Collins, a registered nurse who has been in full-time ministry to cancer patients for eight years, is listed in *Who's Who of American Women* and received the Castleton Sertoma *Service to Mankind Award* in 1980.

Mary Beth Moster, who teaches journalism classes at Indiana University, is the author of several magazine articles as well as two other books.